CW01657754

Tom Cord was within three months of retirement when bushwhack lead cut him down. No lawman ever allowed one of his fellow officers to be murdered without making every effort to get his killer. Deputy Sheriff Bradford Counter, a modern-day gun wizard, had been Tom's partner; Woman Deputy Alice Fayde was Tom's niece.

Together they began the hunt for the old deputy's killer. The search took them across the Rockabye County rangelands, through the slums of Gusher City's Bad Bit and into the upper-crust district of Upton Heights. At last the trail ended, with Brad Counter's gun-skill matched against the two professional killers who shot his partner down.

Books by J. T. Edson

THE REBEL SPY
THE BAD BUNCH
TRAIL BOSS
THE BIG HUNT
THE HARD RIDERS
THE TEXAN
RIO GUNS
THE YSABEL KID
SAGEBRUSH SLEUTH
ARIZONA RANGER
QUIET TOWN
WACO'S DEBT
THE RIO HONDO KID
APACHE RAMPAGE
THE DRIFTER
THE HALF BREED
TERROR VALLEY
MCGRAW'S INHERITANCE
THE FASTEST GUN IN TEXAS
WAGONS TO BACKSIGHT
THE FORTUNE HUNTERS
THE MAN FROM TEXAS
THE TROUBLE BUSTERS
THE BULL WHIP BREED
A TOWN CALLED YELLOWDOG
THE COLT AND THE SABRE
THE LAW OF THE GUN
RETURN TO BACKSIGHT
CALAMITY SPELLS TROUBLE
GUN WIZARD
GUNSMOKE THUNDER
WACO RIDES IN
THE RUSHERS
THE RIO HONDO WAR
TRIGGER FAST
THE WILDCATS
THE PEACEMAKERS
TROUBLED RANGE
SLAUGHTER'S WAY
THE COW THIEVES
GUNS IN THE NIGHT
THE DEVIL GUN
THE FAST GUN
COMANCHE
HOUND DOG MAN
SIDEWINDER
THE FLOATING OUTFIT
TROUBLE TRAIL
RANGELAND HERCULES
THE HOODED RIDERS
THE MAKING OF A LAWMAN
THE PROFESSIONAL KILLERS

J. T. Edson

The Professional Killers

CORGI BOOKS
A DIVISION OF TRANSWORLD PUBLISHERS

THE PROFESSIONAL KILLERS

A CORGI BOOK 552 08048 9

First publication in Great Britain

PRINTING HISTORY
Corgi Edition published 1968

Copyright © J. T. Edson 1968

This book is set in
Baskerville 9/10½ pt.

Corgi Books are published by Transworld Publishers, Ltd.,
Bashley Road, London, N.W.10

Made and printed in Great Britain by
Richard Clay (The Chaucer Press), Ltd., Bungay, Suffolk

For
Graham & Ivy Pouncey

AUTHOR'S NOTE

I would like to thank the Sheriff's Association of Texas and the Texas Department of Public Safety for their invaluable help and information on matters of modern law-enforcement.

CHAPTER ONE

SOME of the old West's trades have gone for ever. The buffalo hunter is no more, departed in the wake of the once enormous herds of bison his rifle decimated. No longer does the prairie scout guide wagon trains or lead avenging troops of cavalry across the plains. Instead of raiding, stealing horses and taking the white-eye brother's scalp, the Indian now goes to college, becomes a business man, truck driver, football star, wrestler or takes to other mundane pursuits. Even the glamorous town marshal is replaced by prosaic, though possibly more efficient, policemen.

Yet others of the old trades remain. Sleath and Jordan came to Gusher City, seat of Rockabye County, Texas, to practise one such trade which had withstood the test of time and retained a niche in the modern, jet-age world. They had come to kill a man; a man neither had ever met and who had done them no harm. Sleath and Jordan followed an old West trade brought up-to-date—they were professional killers.

Bringing the dark blue, four-door Plymouth Fury sedan along Station Street, Sleath swung it neatly into the last parking spot before the corner of Hardin Street, facing the steps leading into the entrance hall of the Southern Pacific Railroad's depot. Glancing at his watch, Sleath saw the time was nine forty-five. He gave a low grunt of satisfaction. Their schedule appeared to be working as planned. With their combined experience, it mostly did.

'We'd best stay here,' he remarked over his shoulder to Jordan. 'The train won't be in for at least five minutes though.'

'Be best,' Jordan replied, his voice breezy and friendly-sounding. 'We've been lucky enough to hit this spot. Leave us no chance lousing the luck by driving round the block. It might be filled when we get back. I hate taking a contract on the fly.'

'I'll feed the parking meter,' Sleath said, ignoring the other's comment and digging into his pants' pocket for a nickel.

Under similar circumstances many a law-abiding citizen would have ignored the meter, taking a chance that no patrolman would come along; or, if one came, be willing to swear he had only just parked and still searched for a coin to pay the required fee. Trying to beat a parking meter out of its just and lawful due offers a harmless outlet for the little touch of larceny which nestles in even the most law-abiding breast.

In view of his chosen profession, Sleath could hardly be classed as a law-abiding citizen. Yet he moved across the car's seat, leaned out of the window, fed his nickel into the parking meter's slot and watched the dial record his payment. Satisfied that he now possessed the legal right to remain parked upon that particular piece of Southern Texas for a period of one hour, Sleath returned to his place behind the Plymouth's wheel and leaned back with the air of one who has done his civic duty and whose conscience is clear.

Sitting in the rear seat, Jordan took out a package of cigarettes, shook two up and passed one forward to Sleath. After lighting his smoke, Jordan settled back and relaxed to wait until the West-bound train brought in their victim.

As usual when awaiting a contract in the area which formed the Old West, Jordan began to compare the way the early hired killers operated with his own outfit's methods. Somehow it never seemed right to him to make a hit from a car—after paying a parking meter's fee—in one of the locations where his trade received its development.

The professional killers of the 1870s rode horse-back into town, received payment on the spot, made their hit in what passed as a fair fight in those days, or by less legal methods. In the latter case, the killer left a string of horses stretched across the country-side to assist in out-running a vengeance-seeking posse. Things were much easier and simpler in those days. Cut a set of telegraph wires and a man knew no word of his coming could be passed ahead to other lawmen.

Times change and so do methods. Sleath and Jordan had

received their orders by telephone; at least he assumed that Sleath had, for they never met except when on a contract. Such a call brought Jordan to Gusher City on Friday evening. After making a brief contact in the men's room at the airport, he and Sleath had gone to different hotels and waited to hear which of the city's quarter of a million inhabitants would be their hit. Not until Sunday afternoon had a voice over a telephone given out the instructions. They were to collect a dark blue Plymouth Fury with local plates from a car park in Greevers, make a study of the kill-zone, pick out their escape route, then wait for the nine-fifty West-bound train to bring them their hit. That and the description of their victim was all that they need to be told. The rest of the contract, their departure from Gusher City and emergency instructions in case of mishap, had been arranged in their first orders. Payment for the contract would reach them after they had returned to their respective homes.

'It's easy so far,' Jordan remarked, blowing a smoke-ring at the roof of the car. 'Can't say I liked the idea of handling a hit on a Sunday evening, but things've come out better than I expected.'

'Sure,' Sleath replied. 'Any other day and we'd been lucky to find ourselves this parking spot. Tonight we have the street to ourselves. Only three hacks in the rank across there, so they aren't expecting many folks off the train. The less passengers, the easier you pick out the pigeon. This thing's going too easy. I don't like it. Remember that Chicago contract we blew?'

'I'm not likely to forget it.'

'That started easily,' Sleath went on worriedly. 'Just like this. Then it loused up.'

'Conditions were different,' Jordan objected. 'Hell, there's not a handful of traffic here. Later there might be, when the movie-houses close. But by that time we'll be at the airport ready to fly back East.'

'I still don't like it!' grunted Sleath.

Nor did Jordan for all his reassuring words. Several aspects of the contract puzzled him; why had there been no photograph of the victim? why the delay even in learning when to make the hit? Small things—but worrying to a man of Jordan's experience. He glanced down to the blanket-covered shape of the Remington Brushmaster shotgun at his feet. While he carried a 9-mm Browning P-35 automatic pistol holstered under his arm, he much preferred the deadly buckshot load of the Brushmaster when making a hit across the width of an average street; the nine balls spread just enough to wipe out any chance of a near miss and at that range sufficient would hit their mark to ensure a kill. Yet he still felt the nagging doubts and worries.

Much the same doubts continued to gnaw at Sleath as he sat smoking behind the steering wheel. While Jordan handled the shooting, he would take care of the escape. Glancing into the rear-view mirror, Sleath watched a car cruise slowly by, then saw a man approaching the car. Not just an ordinary man, but one wearing the dark blue peaked hat and uniform of a Gusher City Police Department patrolman, with a Colt Three-Fifty-Seven revolver hanging in the open-topped holster at his right side; a significant sign in an area which prided itself on the ability of its law-enforcement officers in handling weapons.

'Cop coming,' Sleath said quietly, not turning around.

Neither Jordan nor Sleath showed any anxiety at the thought of a policeman approaching, despite the warning. They did not draw down their hat brims, or raise their coat collars to avoid recognition. It never occurred to Sleath to start the car's engine and drive away. Instead they stayed just as they were, each continuing to smoke and giving no hint that they knew—or had reason to care—about the patrolman's presence.

For his part, the patrolman had not spent twenty years in the G.C.P.D. without learning to perform his duty with as much ease and little inconvenience to himself as possible. He did his work thoroughly, but no longer went out of his way to look for minor infractions on which he might make a pinch. Pinch-hunting was a game for young rookie cops who had not yet learned that each pinch meant extra paperwork and time spent in court, mostly on an off-watch day.

In another part of town, in front of some jewellery or fur store in Business Division, even though the car be legally parked, the patrolman would certainly have stopped and asked questions. However, he saw nothing suspicious in a car parked opposite a railroad depot, especially with a passenger train due to arrive at any moment. Police caution led him to give the car a searching glance, noting licence number, make, colour and the fact that it contained two occupants; the one in the rear tall and bulky, the driver slightly taller and slimmer, both wearing dark slouch hats and what appeared to be dark business suits. A Plymouth Fury had been on the stolen car list, but that was a two-tone, not dark blue. Only one thing remained to be checked. One look at the parking meter's dial told him the fee had been correctly paid, so he passed on without another glance.

During his career as a cop, the patrolman had learned how touchy honest tax-paying citizens could be, especially when seated in a legally-parked car. Stirred by righteous indignation, plus the fact that they had paid out a whole nickel for the privilege of parking, many people objected to too close a scrutiny from a passing patrolman. As a complaint from an indignant tax-payer meant a visit—in off-watch hours—to the House Captain's office for formal explanation and rebuke, a wise cop tried to avoid giving cause for the citizen's wrath.

After passing the Plymouth, the patrolman crossed the junction with Hardin Street. He heard the nine-fifty Westbound draw into the depot but did not bother to wait for it. A short distance along Station Street stood a police telephone and after calling in a routine check on the Plymouth's licence number he aimed to go eat a hot-dog at a near-by stand.

Sleath and Jordan watched the patrolman's departure with relief. Neither wanted to make the hit with a cop so close at hand—especially when the cop be an old hand who wore a Colt 'maggie' and looked like he could be relied upon to act real fast in an emergency. While being professional killers, the two men were not suicidally inclined.

Once more Sleath glanced at his wristwatch. He stubbed out the cigarette in the car's ashtray and then reached down to turn the ignition key. Experience had taught him never to leave starting the motor until the last minute in case it failed to catch at the vital moment. Listening to the purr of the powerful motor, Sleath nodded his satisfaction. When Jordan made the hit, he would be ready to start the car rolling without a second's delay.

Reaching down, Jordan uncovered the Brushmaster and

lifted it from the floor. He examined the gun carefully, working the slide to feed a shell into the chamber. Never had he come across a firearm so ideally suited for his purpose. The Brushmaster balanced well, its twenty-inch barrel carried an adjustable rifle-type rear and ramp foresight instead of the usual shotgun fittings, which greatly increased its accuracy potential. Built to handle buckshot or solid slug loads and used for deer hunting in heavy brush, the gun also met with all Jordan's specialised needs—except one. However, the Brushmaster's one failing had not yet proved any disadvantage and Jordan tended to regard the gun as being lucky.

'Here they come,' Sleath said, taking his attention from the escape-route for a moment and glancing at the entrance to the depot.

'Get set then,' Jordan replied.

Cautiously Jordan raised the Brushmaster, making sure its barrel did not extend through the open window. He did not know what manner of man they waited to kill, but taking precautions cost nothing. Cradling the gun at his shoulder, he lined the sights on the steps, watching the few people who came out of the entrance and down to the street.

After his one quick look, Sleath ignored the entrance and gave his full attention to the impending departure. A check through the rear-view mirror showed him that no traffic approached. Ahead the cop stood some seventy yards away, back to the car, speaking over the official telephone. That could be bad, meaning the hunt would start a few seconds earlier; although Sleath doubted if the few seconds were likely to make any serious difference to their escape. Swiftly he turned the escape-route over in his mind and made sure he knew just where he must go. Gripping the steering wheel in his gloved hands, brakes off, car in gear, powerful engine purring ready for the clutch to be freed. The instant the shotgun boomed, Sleath would be ready to do his part in the contract.

Yet the awaited boom did not come. A few people streamed down the steps, all three cabs departed with fares, men and women walked off along the other side of Station Street—and still the Brushmaster did not roar.

'Somebody goofed!' Jordan growled, lowering the gun as

the last of the passengers emerged and started to take their departure. 'He didn't show.'

'I knew this caper was going too easy,' Sleath complained. 'Just like that Chicago contr——'

'Shut it!' Jordan hissed and brought up his gun again.

A man appeared at the depot entrance and started to walk down the steps. Carefully Jordan studied the latecomer. Just over middle-height, stocky, wearing a black slouch hat, tan belted trenchcoat of a pattern that had gone out of style five years or so previously, carrying a brown suitcase. Each detail matched the description they had been given by their contractor. He was the man whom they had come to Gusher City to kill.

Once more Jordan sighted his Brushmaster. It would not be a difficult shot, far easier than the one which had brought down the ten-pointer whitetail buck that Jordan had taken in the Catskills and had hoped would win itself a place in the Boone & Crockett Club's trophy lists.

With the sights lined, Jordan squeezed the trigger. The gun barked and he felt the recoil-pad thrust back against his shoulder, muzzle-blast momentarily blinded him, and nine .32-calibre balls belched out of the twelve-gauge barrel. Instantly he worked the cocking-slide, ejecting the empty case and feeding a loaded round into the chamber. The move came automatically, needing no thought.

Caught in the chest by several of the buckshot balls, the victim lurched backwards, dropping his case and trying to claw open his trenchcoat, his feet struck the step behind him and he began to fall backwards; Jordan fired again, the second charge ripping home as the victim started to go down.

As the second shot sounded, Sleath started the Plymouth moving, even before Jordan had ejected its empty case. The car picked up speed, swinging around the corner on to Hardin Street, increasing acceleration by the second. Along Station Street the patrolman had dropped the telephone receiver and whirled on hearing the shots. His 'maggie' came into his hand fast, but he did not shoot. Before he could take careful aim—and such would be needed to avoid a miss which might endanger innocent lives—the car had swung on to Hardin and gone from sight.

Sleath flashed one quick look in the patrolman's direction, noticing the speedy reaction and feeling grateful that the man had not been closer. A slight grin creased Sleath's face as his last sight of the patrolman showed the other springing forward. Before the cop reached Hardin, Sleath knew they would be out of sight and range.

'It went off A-o.k. after all,' Jordan stated as Sleath took the car in a tight turn on to a dimly-lit street which crossed Hardin some four blocks below the junction with Station.

'Yeah,' Sleath replied doubtfully. 'Looks that way. But I don't know. I still reckon there's something wrong with this caper.'

CHAPTER TWO

DEPUTY SHERIFF BRADFORD COUNTER stood in the darkness and waited, holding down the feeling of tension which threatened to rise and affect his speed of reaction. Any moment now a light would flicker on for an instant, while its control switch was worked back and forward. In that brief flash of illumination he must see his mark, draw his gun, shoot and make a hit.

On came the light, some seven yards away from where Brad stood and slightly to his left. Its momentary glow showed a life-sized man-shaped buff target with an X-ring in the centre of the chest area. The light also illuminated Brad: an exceptionally handsome young man with curly, golden blond hair, six foot three inches in height, one hundred and ninety-five pounds stripped and with the build of the muscle-men heroes of Italian epic movies. Brad wore a dark blue sharkskin shirt, open at the neck and sporting a yellow silk cravat, dark grey flannel slacks and black, crepe-soled Sears-Roebuck kangaroo leather boots. Around his waist hung an official pattern gun-belt, two and a half inches broad to support the weight it carried, with handcuff pouch and container for spare ammunition at the left side. The right side supported a high-riding, forward raked, steel-lined skimpy Bianchi Cooper-Combat holster incorporating the Elden Carl fly-off safety strap to hold Brad's Colt Government Model .45 automatic in place during normal wear, yet still permitting a *very* rapid withdrawal of the weapon.

The gun was no snub-nosed hide-out weapon, lacking in both power and accuracy; nor was it merely the fine mechanism which came off the Colt factory's production lines. On purchasing the gun, Brad had sent it to the Pachmayr Gun

Works in Los Angeles with instructions that it be accurised. This entailed tightening the fit between the cocking-slide and receiver, installing an enlarged bushing, decreasing barrel-slackness and improving the accuracy potential. The internal mechanism was worked over to give smoother functioning. To ensure quicker and more certain transfer of bullets from the magazine to the chamber, the feed ramp was polished to an icy slickness and the barrel's mouth so trimmed that a round could pass over the joint effortlessly and without jamming. Externally the gun possessed combat stocks shaped to make certain Brad's fingers always closed on it in the same manner. The butt's grip safety had been welded into the 'fire' position and the manual safety catch enlarged for easier slipping into a condition of readiness. A trigger-shoe shoe spread the four pounds pressure necessary to fire the gun, giving the impression of a lighter pull to a squeezing finger without loss of safety margin. Finally the gun carried an adjustable rear sight to give increased accuracy.

To make the most of his gun's advantages, Brad did not use the normal round-nosed service ammunition. For work he filled his magazines with heavy-duty hand-loaded, base-jacketed, truncated cone-shaped bullets of the type designed by the master of combat shooting, Jeff Cooper. Such bullets boosted the .45 automatic to 70.1 on the Hatcher Scale of Relative Stopping Power—which gauges various handgun calibres on their ability to produce an instant, one-shot hit on a human being—and put it third in line after the 76.3 of the .45 Single Action Army Colt and the thumb-busting 142.8 rating of the great .44 Magnum. Far above the 30.8 scored by the .38 Special snub-nosed revolvers many detectives were forced by their departments to carry for their protection.

While all the improvements did not put the big Colt in the same target class as an Olympic free-pistol, they turned it into the finest fighting handgun ever made. With that accurised Colt in his hands, using one or another of the braced-holds devised by combat masters, Brad could perform shooting of a kind usually only done by western movie heroes—except that Brad used live ammunition in his gun.

The light showed Brad his target briefly then was gone, throwing his weight on to his heels, Brad leaned his upper torso slightly backwards as his right hand flicked up towards the holster. Hooking his forefinger under the long tang of the fly-off strap, Brad released it from the retaining stud. Having been held in position against tension, the strap shot into the air on its release, the loop sliding from under the hammer and leaving all ready for use.

Fast though Brad reacted, he moved in pitch darkness as he speed-rocked the gun from leather. So perfect had the drill become that Brad neither slipped his forefinger into the triggerguard nor placed his thumb on the safety catch until the gun had cleared his holster and slanted towards where he had remembered seeing the target illuminated.

Barely had the light gone out when flame tore from Brad's gun barrel and the crash of the shot merged with a dull clang. The sound told Brad his bullet had scored a hit, even before a voice boomed out of the blackness behind him.

'Target One!' it announced. 'Hit!'

'One down and five to go,' Brad thought, applying the safety catch and holstering the Colt; although he let the fly-off strap lie where it had landed. 'Can I do it?'

So far nobody had ever gone clean—made the maximum score—on all three stages of the 'Night Shoot', one of combat shooting's hardest tests. Brad had fired the course many times, with a high score of twenty-eight out of thirty hits, twenty of which had been in the X-ring, and at different times managed to go clean on all three stages; yet he never could manage to make the elusive three straight under competition stresses and conditions.

On this occasion Brad had gone clean on the first stage; firing six shots from ten yards at an illuminated target, reloading and firing a further six in the dark—testing his ability to shoot accurately under an uncontrolled source of light, reload and re-engage the target with memory and body-orientation as the means of locating its position—the whole to be completed in fourteen seconds, the first four of which only were illuminated.

Nor had the second stage cost him any points. Starting at ten yards, in darkness and with his gun holstered, then engaging a line of three targets which he pinpointed by means of an electric torch held in his left hand. On both of the strings fired he hit each target twice in the four seconds allowed by the rules.

Now Brad faced the final stage. Seven yards away in the blackness stood a line of six targets, each to be individually illuminated at random and by a mere flick of a light switch. Once seen, Brad only needed to draw, shoot at and hit the designated target—in the dark.

Brad normally reckoned the last to be easiest of the three stages. Usually it would have been; but not when following his old shooting rival, Sam Allardyce, pride of the Presidio County sheriff's office, after Sam had shot twenty-nine out of the thirty and put twenty-one of them in the X-ring. Sam had wiped Brad's eye by a couple of points gathered running the Mexican Defence Course to win the Sheriffs' Association of Texas's Leatherslap Contest earlier that year and Brad hoped to snatch a victory on the Night Shoot to even the score.

Despite the thrill of competition, combat shooting was not a stunt, a silly childish game, nor an attempt to act like a television cowboy. There were times, even in the jet-age, when a lawman's life depended on the speed of his draw and accuracy in placing home his bullets. Down on the Rio Grande where narcotics smugglers ran their hateful cargoes across the river from Mexico was but one occasion when a peace officer needed his gun—and not for a movie stunt. Being all too aware of that fact, Brad maintained his drawing speed and shooting eye at a high level. He was funny like that, he wanted to stay alive.

Three more times the light winked on, showing him the next target, each exposure being followed by the crash of his automatic an instant after darkness descended again on the scene. On each occasion the sound of the shot received punctuation in the form of lead clanging against target-steel.

Four down and two to go! Brad felt the tension rising inside him and fought to hold it in check. With a chance of the fabulous three-straight so close, he must not allow himself to tighten and goof the last couple of shots. Time seemed to be standing still as Brad waited for the next exposure.

It did not come. Instead the range officer's voice boomed hollowly through the blackness.

'Brad. You're wanted on the telephone. I'm putting on the main lights—now.'

A low grunt of annoyance burst from Brad. When a man built himself up to a peak in preparation for a great physical and mental effort—and combat shooting takes as much of both as any other strenuous sport needs—he did not take kindly to having his concentration ruined.

On giving the word 'now', after a brief pause to allow Brad to settle his alerted muscles so they would not react to the glow, the range officer switched on the main lights and illuminated the long building used for close-range target work. Ahead of Brad, six targets stood before the back-stop, four of them showed marks of his bullets.

Although seething with rage, Brad made no attempt to turn from the firing line until he had put his weapon in a safe condition. Setting the safety catch down into the 'safe' position, he holstered the Colt. Then he bent and picked up the fly-off strap, slipping the loop under the Colt's drawn-back hammer and pressing home the retainer stud. With all safe he turned and walked back along the range. Some thirty men, members of the Rockabye County Combat Club and Sam Allardyce's supporters—most of them law-enforcement officers of one kind or another—stood or sat on the rear of the firing line. Sam, big, burly, yet light on his feet, and the Presidio section all grinned.

'Nice timing, Brad boy,' Sam remarked. 'Knew you couldn't lick me and fixed to have a call put through to you.'

'I bet it's that blonde I saw you with last week at the Lido Club, Brad,' a member of the Gusher City Police Department's Narcotics Squad called.

'She'll be sorry if it is,' Brad growled back.

Yet he doubted if the blonde would be calling him. While she might not be rated among the world's great intellects, the girl knew a damned sight better than make telephone calls to him while he was engaged in combat shooting—or if she did not, she sure as hell soon would. Promising himself to ruin what could develop into a beautiful friendship if it should be the blonde, Brad passed through the crowd and entered the range officer's sound-proofed cubicle by the main doors. He closed the cubicle door behind him, not wanting to give Presidio the wrong impression of Rockabye County's gentlemanly behaviour by allowing them to overhear his comments if it happened to be the blonde on the line.

'Counter here,' he growled into the receiver of the telephone, sounding as menacing as a winter-starved silvertip grizzly waking and finding a picnic party in its den-cave.

'Brad!' replied a male voice so strained with tension and emotion that he barely recognised it. 'This's Sam Cuchilo—I've bad news——'

Ten seconds later Brad had forgotten the blonde, his thoughts on the subject of folks ruining his concentration and his desire to make the three-straight. The words crackling over the telephone wires to his ears shook him brutally and he could understand why Deputy Sheriff Sam Cuchilo, that usually unemotional full-blood Comanche Indian college-graduate, sounding so strange and slightly incoherent.

'My God!' Brad gasped. 'When, and where?'

'Not five minutes ago. I'm on watch at the office and the call was relayed over the hot-shot speaker. It was down at the depot on Station Street, out front of the main entrance.'

'I'll go straight over. Thanks, Sam.'

He hung up without further speech. Having heard all he needed to, Brad did not want to waste any more of Sam Cuchilo's, or his own, time.

Replacing the receiver, Brad leaned for a moment on the desk, allowing his churned-up feelings to have their violent race before trying to regain control. With the spasm passed, he took out the big automatic, removed its magazine and then worked the slide to kick out the cartridge from the chamber. Taking a reserve magazine from his belt pouch, he ran a thumb over the top bullet. Unlike the ejected round, the bullet carried a head shaped like a truncated cone. Thrusting home the magazine with its heavy-duty bullets into the butt housing, Brad drew back and released the slide to feed the top round into the chamber. After setting the safety, he holstered and secured the gun. Sucking in a deep breath, Brad pocketed the discarded magazine and round. Then he walked out of the room.

It said much for Brad's self-control that his face showed nothing of the shock brought by the message. Every eye turned towards him and the men, most of them schooled in the art of reading facial expressions, read nothing from his features.

'Are you shooting again tonight, Brad?' asked the range officer.

'Not tonight,' Brad answered, fighting to hold his voice steady. 'I have to leave right now.'

'She can't be *that* impatient, Brad,' put in the man who suggested the blonde as a possible interruption to the business of the evening.

'Chasing women, for shame,' grinned Allardyce. 'You ought to keep your eye in, Brad. A lawman never knows when he's likely to need a gun.'

'I may need to know real soon,' Brad answered. 'Tom Cord's just been shot and killed.'

The words brought a sudden descent of shocked silence. Most of the men present had known and liked Deputy Sheriff Tom Cord and all were aware that Tom had been Brad's partner. While the men knew Brad to be something of a practical joker, he always took combat shooting in the correct manner, as a deadly serious subject; and no lawman *ever* joked about his partner being killed.

After watching Brad leave the range, two of the men exchanged glances. They were detectives on the G.C.P.D. and, although both had a wife and family awaiting their return, knew they would report to their respective station houses in case they might be needed. Silently they left the room and the other local officers prepared to make their departure.

'That's all for tonight, boys,' the range officer announced quietly. 'Let's clean up and close shop.'

'You local badges'd best get going,' Allardyce put in. 'We'll stop on and tend to things here.'

On leaving the building, Brad walked across the parking lot to where his imported M.G. MGB convertible stood waiting. Despite the M.G., the fact that he lived in an apartment on snob Upton Heights, dressed fashionably and expensively, and spent at least fifteen dollars a week on training ammunition, Brad was not a corrupt, bribe-taking officer. Born into one of Texas' richest families, he might have been employed by the Counter Oil Company, run their big ranch or joined one or another of the various subsidiary interests of his kin; but some desire, instinct, call it what you will, drove him to become a deputy sheriff. Possibly it stemmed back to the blood of his great-grandfather. Mark Counter had been one of the old-time gun wizards and, if all the legends be true, quite a man in his day.[1]

Whatever his reasons, Brad gave up a sinecure in the family business empire. First he majored in Police Science and Administration at the University of Southern Texas and then, with some assistance from his maternal grandfather, took the F.B.I.'s twelve week police officers' training course. With that behind him, Brad applied for a post as deputy under Jack Tragg, the sheriff of Rockabye County. Brad had been a deputy for over a year. In the early days he tried maybe a mite too hard, feeling he must prove to the other officers that he gained his post on merit and not through the good offices of the Counter millions. Brad took more than his fair share of the dull office routine, the boring stints as court bailiff, serving out writs, and sitting through lonely, miserable stake-outs in areas where the waiting was done under a tree or crouched in a clump of mesquite instead of in the relative comfort of a car or undercover truck.

Three months back Brad had helped Jack Tragg to run down a vicious gang engaged in bringing illegal immigrants across the border, and while cracking the case had also trapped a mighty smart smuggler. After that Brad had no longer needed to prove himself to anybody—not even to Bradford Counter.

Brad did not discount what he owed to Tom Cord for his success. Tom had always been helpful, ready with advice and eager to pass on the wisdom gained in many years of law enforcement. Despite the difference in their ages, they had been close friends. Now Tom lay dead, shot down like a dog. Brad swore he would get the killer.

Cold, controlled anger throbbed through Brad as he drove the M.G. out of the parking lot and swung west along the track bordering the large, well-equipped ranges of the Rockabye County Shooting Club. A mile ahead glowed the lights of Gusher City and somewhere in the sprawling county seat was the man who had killed Tom Cord.

Keeping the M.G. at a steady forty, Brad reached the edge

[1] *Mark Counter's story is recorded in the author's Floating Outfit novels.*

of town. A black and white radio patrol car of the G.C.P.D. cut out of a side valley and after him. Knowing better than to try to out-run the R.P., even though the matter be urgent, he brought the M.G. to a halt. The R.P. drew alongside and stopped, its shotgun—the local term for the crew member not at the steering wheel—started to climb out.

'All right, lead boot,' he began, 'where at's th——'

Taking out his identification wallet, Brad held it so the shotgun could see the enclosed deputy's badge and official ID card.

'Counter, Deputy Sheriff,' he said. 'I want "code three" cover to the depot on Station Street.'

Instantly the patrolman's slightly aggressive attitude changed. While he objected to Upton Heights' bloods careering through town in their fancy imported sports cars—probably because he could not afford one and disliked seeing folks enjoying leisure hours while he worked—the shotgun had been listening to his radio and knew the reason for the big blond deputy's haste in reaching Station Street. A deputy sheriff in Rockabye County held equivalent rank to lieutenant of the Patrol Bureau; but even without the disciplinary pull the patrolman would have been only too pleased to help out under the circumstances.

'Start that heap, sir,' he ordered, jerking his head back into the R.P. 'Get rolling, Stan.'

A few seconds later Brad's M.G. raced through the quiet streets, the Sunday night's traditional calm split by the wailing of the R.P.'s siren as its flashing red light gave out a 'code three' warning to all traffic that they must give way to the two vehicles speeding across town on urgent business.

CHAPTER THREE

Looking along Station Street as he approached the depot in the wake of the R.P., Brad saw the familiar scene that he had come to associate with any homicide. Only this was not just any homicide. A good friend lay dead at the centre of the attraction. Brad had never been so intimately connected with a killing as he was in this murder of his partner and friend.

The R.P. halted beyond the crowd of spectators who stood in a huddled group of the sidewalk. Turning, the car's crew looked back to where Brad had stopped his M.G.

"Want to go in closer?' called the shotgun.

'I'll walk on in,' Brad answered, swinging from the M.G. 'Thanks for getting me here so quick.'

'That's all right. We hope you get the bastard.'

Having delivered that sentiment, the shotgun withdrew his head and the driver swung their car in a U-turn to drive off in the direction from which they came. Brad raised a hand in a salute as the car went by, then he walked along the street.

A small knot of people stood with their backs to him, watched over by a brace of patrolmen as they waited for developments. Three R.P.s and a black and white sheriff's office Oldsmobile Super 88 deputy car filled spaces on the parking zone where the killers had waited for their victim. Before the steps an ambulance stood white and slightly sinister in such a setting, its crew already loading a sheet-draped form on a stretcher through the open rear doors. A black detective's car parked ahead of the ambulance, two men Brad recognised stood by it, one of them speaking into the vehicle's transmission microphone. Beyond the entrance to the depot, held back by more patrolmen, a second crowd stared, pointed and muttered in muted tones at each new development.

Even as Brad showed one of the guardian patrolmen his ID

and walked by, a white-coated medical examiner joined the two men at the black D car, handed one a slip of paper, returned to the ambulance and climbed aboard to drive away. Halting for a moment, Brad watched the ambulance glide silently by. Inside it lay the body of his good friend, headed for the M.E.'s room where the autopsy would be performed; as always when a violent or unattended death took place.

Brad fought to prevent any emotion showing as he walked on. It was not his first contact with violent death. He had been forced to kill a man on his first day as a deputy and had slowly adjusted himself to the unpleasant realisation that taking another human being's life occasionally formed part of a peace officer's duty. The man Brad had killed that day had been a badly wanted murderer with at least two deaths to his credit, and had been shooting at Brad when the young deputy's lead had cut him down. So Brad felt little about killing—or as little as a thinking man could when forced to the ultimate of taking another human being's life. The present case was different. No matter how Brad tried to tell himself otherwise, he knew he was involved deeply—perhaps too deeply.

Standing by the D car, cradling the microphone in one big hand, Deputy Ian Grantley gave Brad a nod, but continued to spit out his orders. 'Road block fixed at junction of Main Highway 90 and State Auto Road 127, roger, Ted. Cen-Con, make sure Laslo detachment cover 118 as well as the Juarez Bridge. Notify Captain Garcia to be on look-out for dark blue, four door Plymouth Fury sedan, local plates, 176524. Two occupants believed white, male, American, both tall, one slim, other heavily-built, they are armed and dangerous.'

'Brad,' greeted Grantley's partner, Deputy Jake Melnick; a tall, slim, dark and serious-looking young man who rarely smiled and yet managed to look even less jovial at that moment. 'We've put Operation Close-Off into full force.'

'Thanks, Jake,' Brad replied, then looked to where Grantley lowered the microphone. 'I'll take it, Ian.'

Grantley threw a long, searching look at Brad's face, then swung his eyes to his partner. The same question rose in each man's mind. Could a green deputy, even one who showed considerable promise and was the best all-round gun-handler in the sheriff's office, take on so serious an investigation. Yet, as

Tom's partner, Brad could expect to be placed in charge of the case.

'What's been done so far?' Brad continued without waiting for the other two to confirm or refuse his request.

'Patrolman Schuster reported the—the killing,' Grantley answered; even such a hard-bitten old hand found it difficult to stay calm and formal when death struck so close to him. 'Schuster had passed the car a few minutes before. It was correctly parked, the meter paid, so he didn't pay much attention. Got the number though, I've relayed it to D.M.V., and thinks the occupants to be two males, white, both tall, wearing dark slouch hats and darkish business suits. Can't get it any closer than that. He recognised Tom and called in. We've started Operation Close-Off. Airport, railroad and bus depots covered, Border Patrol alerted, road-blocks in place.'

Rockabye County might be one of the largest in Texas and, with the oil-wells pouring out their Texas-tea, one of the richest, but there were few ways out of town that could not be effectively covered. The State Auto Road ran north to connect with Main Highway 90. A few second and lower-grade roads traversed the ninety-five mile length and one hundred and fifty mile width of the county. All could be, and already were, under observation. The Rio Grande formed the county's southern boundary and the two bridges which crossed had alert, watchful men on them. Of course the killers might go across country, or along a river track, ditching their car and travelling on foot. Below the border Captain Garcia of the Mexican Police ran a very efficient organisation and no two *gringos* could move far in his territory without word reaching him of their presence. If caught below the border the two men would be quietly returned to U.S. soil; part of a strictly unofficial arrangement between Jack Tragg and Garcia under which each returned the other's wanted nationals across the international border without the delay and formality of official extradition processes.

Helicopters of the sheriff's air patrol stood by. At the airport, the G.C.P.D.'s Flight Detail moved swiftly into action. Keen-eyed men scrutinised every passenger at the airport and anybody carrying a box or case long enough to contain a shotgun was politely but firmly requested to open up for a search. Just as keen a watch covered the city's railroad and bus depots, and police cars scoured the streets, looking for the Plymouth.

No call ever received such prompt attention as when a lawman had been the victim of a killing. *Esprit de corps* alone did not account for the urgency. Any man who killed a policeman in cold blood was the most dangerous type of criminal and would not hesitate to cut down anybody who stood in his way.

Turning, Brad looked towards the steps. A chalk outline marked where the old deputy fell, the red stain was his life blood. Letting out a long sigh, Brad swung back in time to see a police photographer approach Grantley. The burly, red-haired detective nodded in Brad's direction and it was to the big blond that the technician handed the results of his work; a sheaf of freshly developed Land Polaroid photographs of the scene of the crime.

'They used a shotgun,' Brad said in a low voice, studying the photographs and trying to keep the impersonal note in his voice.

'Yes,' Melnick agreed, taking an envelope from his pocket. 'I found the shot-wads while measuring the street.'

A big black Buick came along the street as Brad took the envelope. The car bore Department of Motor Vehicles licence plates and carried a built-in red blinker light on the front windscreen. Stepping forward, one of the patrolmen handling the far crowd threw open the Buick's door and tossed a salute to the man who stepped out. While the car belonged to Chief of Police Phineas Hagen, it was the sheriff not the head of the G.C.P.D. who emerged.

Clad in a black tuxedo, Jack Tragg still gave the impression of the tall, tanned, traditional Western lawman. He stood six foot one, with close-cropped black hair and a sun-bronzed face which had the rugged charm of the outdoor man. Ignoring the flash bulbs of press cameras and the attempt by a couple of local reporters to throw questions at him, Jack walked to where his deputies stood. Unlike the majority of Texas, Rockabye County maintained its sheriff as a permanent officer and placed him as supreme head of all local law enforcement in the county. No law-abiding citizen could fault the system or claim that Jack Tragg did not give the tax-payers value for their money. Shrewd, efficient, capable, he ran the county's law and maintained a happy balance with Chief Hagen who commanded a major city's Police Department.

After glancing at the chalk outline for a moment, his lips working in soundless words that might have been a prayer, Jack joined his waiting deputies.

'Who has it?' he asked without wasting time on preliminaries.

A slight pause followed the sheriff's words. Technically only the senior deputy present had the right to answer the question. Grantley, as senior man, made his decision fast.

'Brad,' he said.

'All right, Brad,' Jack went on, confirming Grantley's decision. 'How much's been done?'

'I've only just arrived,' Brad replied. 'Close-Off's in operation, all informed, the local work's being tied up——'

'Rudert and Klein from Headquarters are asking questions among the kibitzers and I sent a R.P. along Hardin,' Grantley finished for Brad.

At that moment one of the G.C.P.D. detectives returned, a tall, bronzed man Brad thought he recognised accompanying him. Grantley jerked a thumb in Brad's direction as the detective steered his charge that way.

'Brad has it now,' Grantley said. 'He was Tom's partner.'

'Huh huh!' grunted the detective. 'This's Mr Carter——'

'Hi there, Brad,' greeted the witness, stepping past his escort. 'Damned bad business this. You may not remember——'

'I've shot skeet against you at the Club,' Brad interrupted. 'Did you see what happened?'

'Not much of it. The wife was supposed to be on the nine-fifty and I stood in the hall waiting until everybody left. The feller—the one who was shot, he was last out. I'd seen the car, never gave it much attention though. Then I saw the muzzle-blast and heard the shots. Came from the back seat, with the barrel inside the car, not poking through the window. Twelve gauge, I'd say from the sound and flame. And, going on the time lapse between the shots, I'd guess at a single barrel pump gun.'

'Could you be sure of that?' Grantley asked.

'Not to swear to in court,' Carter admitted. 'But I'm pretty fair with a shotgun and the time lag between the shots struck me as being about right for a good man handling the pump of a single barrel.'

'You didn't see what either of the men in the car looked like?' Brad inquired, making the routine question automatically.

'No, but one of your cops walked by it——'

'We've got his story,' Grantley grunted. 'Car was legally parked and——'

'No offence, Deputy,' Carter said. 'I know how the cop thought and don't blame him. Say, one thing struck me though.'

'What's that?' asked a mollified Grantley.

'The smooth way the driver got his heap rolling right after the shooting. It looked like real good team-work to me.'

'Schuster remarked on that, Brad,' Melnick put in.

'Huh huh,' Brad acknowledged, docketing the information and turning to Carter. 'Thanks for your help, Frank. We might want to get in touch.'

'I'll be around,' Carter promised, and returned to the crowd.

'Can we rely on him, Brad?' Jack asked. 'His guess about the gun, I mean.'

'He's a shotgun nut, Jack,' Brad replied, and even in his grief at the loss of Tom Cord could not resist going on, 'and they're even worse than revolver-cranks.'

Jack and Grantley exchanged satisfied nods. Many a heated discussion had raged among the deputies on the relative merits of revolver and automatic pistol as a combat weapon, with Brad defending automatics vehemently. If he could make his usual dig at revolver-users, Brad would be all right in the handling of the case.

'Put it on the air then, Ian,' Jack ordered. 'Suspects may be armed with pump-action shotgun.'

'Yo!' Grantley replied and returned to the D car to relay a piece of information which might save some policeman's life if he came across the killers. A pump-action shotgun carried five shells as opposed to the two in a double barrelled weapon.

'Anything I can be doing, Brad?' asked Melnick.

'Can you try to learn why Tom waited until last before leaving the depot?'

'I'll make a stab at it.'

Watching Brad and listening to his request, Jack Tragg gave a slight nod. This was the testing time for the young deputy, his moment of truth, when he must either prove himself—justifying Jack's decision to hire him—or fall by the wayside. Certainly Brad appeared to be steady enough and thinking objectively; the crack about revolver-cranks and his request to Melnick proved that.

'I have the wife in the car, Brad,' Jack said. 'We'll go break the news to Mavis Cord. Finish here, then go back to the office and start things moving there.'

The second detective came up with news that none of his section of the crowd could give assistance in the case.

'Unless you want us for anything around here, Rudy and I'll prowl for a spell,' he finished.

'Thanks,' Brad replied.

At normal times some rivalry existed between the G.C.P.D. Detective Bureau and the sheriff's office. Because of their county-wide jurisdiction, Jack and Hagen ruled the deputies based on Gusher City, acted as the area's Homicide Squad, a decision which did not meet with the approval of the majority of detectives. The murder of a deputy cancelled inter-departmental rivalry. Rudert and Klein were willing to continue working on the case all night in the hope of digging up some fact that might help bring Tom's killers to book.

Watching the detectives walk to their car, Brad became aware of the responsibility he bore and the enormity of the task which lay ahead of him. On previous murder investigations, Tom Cord stood at his side, ready to give advice and throw in the weight of his years of experience. Now Brad faced the task of commanding his first major investigation alone—with his friend as the victim.

Brad knew he could rely on the full co-operation of every peace officer in the county, and beyond its boundaries should that become necessary. Nor would he be working alone. One of the other deputies would be assigned to assist him. That brought up another point. All the deputies working from the county's four sub-offices and the main office in Gusher City operated in regular two-man teams. Good team co-ordination could make or break an investigation, but it did not come in a day. Brad wondered who he should ask to partner him on the case.

'Want any more here, Brad?' Grantley asked as the D car drew away.

Before Brad could reply, Melnick returned. 'Tom stopped on talking with Dooley of the Depot Detail, nothing important, just passing the time of day.'

'Thanks, Jake. Let's get back to the office.'

'Sure. Do you want to come in our car?'

'I've got my own heap here,' Brad replied.

'We'll see you back there then,' Grantley stated, and joined his partner to collect the Oldsmobile.

Brad stood alone on the pavement, the sheaf of photographs still held in his hand. Already the crowd, sensing that nothing further would develop, began to scatter. Knowing the local peace officers, the newspapermen headed for the sheriff's office to collect the Public Relations Bureau hand-outs instead of wasting time trying to question the officers involved.

Slowly Brad dropped his eyes to the chalk outline and patch of dark colour which stained the steps. By morning the Department of Sanitation's street-washing units would have washed the chalk and blood away, leaving no sign that a man died on that spot.

Throwing off the thought, Brad gave a last look around. He called over one of the patrolmen and told him to resume his watch, then walked back to the M.G. No more could be done at the scene of the crime, so he must make for the sheriff's office and start organising every available asset in the hunt for Tom Cord's killers.

CHAPTER FOUR

No longer did the Rockabye County sheriff work out of an adobe shack on Main Street. Instead he shared a modern, six storey building with the Headquarters Division of the G.C.P.D.

Brad left his M.G. in the municipal employees' parking lot, crossed Randel Street and entered the front doors of the Department of Public Safety Building. Crossing the entrance hall, he rode the elevator to the third floor, stepping out into the old familiar scene. Facing the elevator doors, a double flight of stairs led up and down. To the right of the stairs lay the sheriff's office records' room, unlit as yet. Next was the comfortable room used by visitors while waiting for service. Lastly came the men's locker room. Three doors graced the left side of the stairs, two bearing the grim legend 'FIREARMS INVESTIGATION LABORATORY. STRICTLY NO ADMITTANCE', a pointless warning as not only were the doors locked and bolted from the inside, but heavy, well-loaded metal cabinets stood in place to keep them shut. The third door, nearest the stairs, bore the F.I.L.. inscription without the prohibitive warning. One could enter that room provided one kept to the visitor's side of the dividing rail and did not waste Lieutenant Jed Cornelius' and his three-man squad's valuable time. The busy attitude of F.I.L. was not a pose. when not engaged in firearms investigation, the four men found plenty of work in reloading ammunition for use in the county's extensive training programme.

Facing F.I.L. were Jack Tragg's office, the watch commander's room and the deputies' squadroom. On the other side of the elevators one found an interrogation room, specially built to protect its users from abuses and false accusations, the Missing Persons Bureau and lastly a small room with 'MEN'S' painted on the door.

On entering the squadroom, Brad found all the fourteen local male deputies and one of the female officers present. The Gusher City Office worked a two-watch rota, from eight in the morning to four in the afternoon and four until midnight. If officers were needed on a case after midnight, Headquarters Division's Business Office called them from their homes. Usually only the eight members of the night watch—less such as might be out on a case—would have been present, but the killing of a fellow officer brought in the off-watch personnel to lend a hand.

Silence lay heavily on the room. Big Pat Rafferty's breezy brogue did not sound, nor did his partner, Tom Chu, use his Hollywood 'B' movie Chinese accent. For once Tony Valenca forgot to bend everybody's ear with comments on the latest television show and huge Lars Larsen slumped in his creaking chair, drumming fingers the size of well-developed bananas on the desk top.

Woman Deputy Joan Hilton came to her feet and walked to meet Brad. Catty comments from the Bureau of Women Officers claimed Joan's blonde hair depended on bottled aid to hide the grey streaks. Certainly her face showed signs of middle-age when seen close-up, but her figure, clad in a uniform blouse and khaki skirt, while plump, looked firm. More than one drunken hooker, 'b' girl or female crook had learned to her sorrow that Joan's arms and legs packed hard muscles and could move with surprising speed when necessary.

'Sorry to hear about it, Brad,' she said. 'I'll fetch a cup of coffee for you, if you like.'

'Thanks, Joan,' Brad replied.

Shortly after Joan left, her opposite number on Brad's watch entered the squadroom. Woman Deputy Alice Fayde's face held a fixed, schooled expression, but grief-lines showed on it. Her red hair, done in a flip-style which looked neat and stylish while being easy to keep that way, framed a face which if not ravingly beautiful bore a rich, warm charm. Not that Alice was a crow. On any street one might find a few better looking girls, but there would be many far less attractive. She stood five foot seven in height and for the rest, in movie star terms, went thirty-seven, twenty-five, thirty-five. A uniform blouse, official slacks and pumps clothed her rich, shapely body, she carried her tunic over her left arm. Hung over her right shoulder, a Pete Ludwig policewoman's bag carried the normal feminine items, plus her ID wallet, handcuff pouch and holstered Colt Cobra .38 Special revolver.

She had been Tom Cord's niece and practically raised by the deputy after the death of her parents. Although she now lived in an apartment at the Chadwick Building on the fringes of Lasher Division, Alice rarely missed a weekly visit to her aunt and uncle's place in Evans Hill.

'Hello, Alice,' Brad greeted, watching her hang up the coat.

'Brad,' she replied, her voice carrying an attractive Southern drawl. 'Joan called me, I called in my place to change before I came over. Has anybody gone to tell Aunt Mavis?'

'Jack and his missus.'

'Good,' she breathed, knowing how capably Mrs Tragg could handle such a delicate matter. 'What's been done?'

'Come and sit down, I'll tell you.'

Taking seats at the desk Tom and he used, Brad began to put Alice in the picture, knowing she could understand every move made. In fact Alice probably knew more about the routine than Brad did. She had been a member of the G.C.P.D.'s Bureau of Women Officers for seven years, from her twenty-first birthday, rising to detective sergeant before transferring to the sheriff's office six months ago. Since her arrival she had proved herself to be a highly competent and efficient officer with a thorough knowledge of all the office's routine. Brad knew her to be a black belt at judo, competent in karate, able to handle herself in a rough-house. She also shot 'Expert' on the County's exacting qualification course; which included combat work far more than formal target-popping.

Just as Brad finished filling Alice and the listening deputies in, the main doors opened and three men entered. Brad put aside the coffee Joan brought him and turned his attention to the trio of men who ran the office. At the forward point of the human triangle stood Jack Tragg. On his left, tall, gaunt and craggy, First Deputy McCall gave the impression of having stepped out of the portrait of a Highland shepherd. A Stetson sat on his head. Nobody in the office could recall having seen him without a hat—rumour held not even McCall's wife had as he slept in it. With or without head-dress, McCall was a shrewd lawman and a damned good watch commander.

To the right, seeming dwarfed by the other two, First Deputy Ricardo Alvarez, night watch commander, looked like a Latin matinee idol and moved with the grace of a bull-fighter. In a sense that was an apt description, with his know-ledge of judo and karate, Alvarez had tamed bulls of men. Unlike the other two, he wore khaki uniform and a .45 Colt Commander automatic pistol rode in a combat bikini holster at his right side.

A silence that could almost be felt dropped on the room as the assembled officers waited for Jack's orders. Yet he did not seem in any hurry to start speaking.

Standing with his left fist snapping into his right palm, legs braced apart, Jack looked across the squadroom. Only he did not see the double line of desks, the filing cabinets, bulletin board, duty roster boards, the hot-shot speaker over the party door leading to the watch commander's office, or the two boxes flanking the door. Instead Jack saw the entrance hall to a stately house in Upton Heights. It had been at the end of the long fight to clean organised crime from Rockabye County and Jack had led a raid on Gus Meyer's home. As senior mem-ber of the party, Jack had gone in first and found himself under the barrel of a Thompson submachine-gun in the hands of a hopped-up young killer on the stairs. Even as death stared Jack in the face, Tom Cord had flung himself forward, knock-ing the sheriff—he had been Captain of Detectives then—side-ways, risking his life to save Jack. Luckily the Thompson's lead missed and before the punk could correct his aim, Tom and Jack's bullets had cut him down. Jack Tragg owed Tom Cord his life. A man of character, such as the sheriff of Rock-abye County, did not soon forget such an act. Now Tom had fallen victim to killer's lead and Jack did not care for the thought.

'I want the bastards who killed Tom,' he told the waiting room.

They waited for more, but Jack had said all he aimed to on the subject. He did not waste time telling them of the necessity of nailing a lawman's killers, for they all knew that without needing a reminder. Nor did he make speeches about the tragic loss of a damned good man, they were all aware of the loss and did not need him to stress the point. So Jack made all the speech he considered necessary in good, old-fashioned Texan and without mincing his words.

'Who do you want with you, Brad?' asked McCall. As the big blond's watch commander it fell on him to allocate a partner, but he left the selection to Brad.

Rising to her feet, Alice faced the trio of her superiors before Brad could ask for Sam Cuchilo to be transferred from the other watch.

'I'll work with him,' she announced.

Every eye turned to her, yet nobody spoke for a good thirty seconds after she made her suggestion. Women deputies mainly handled dispatch work from the Central Control radio room, or attended to business concerning their own sex and juveniles. In every aspect of her work Alice had proved her competence. However, the men wondered if she could take on a homicide case, especially with an inexperienced youngster like Brad as her partner.

'You, Alice?' Jack finally said.

'Why not?' she answered, and the words came boiling hotly out of her mouth. 'The objection *is* because I'm a woman, isn't it?' She paused, waiting for somebody to speak and when nobody did, went on, 'I *am* a woman, but nobody throws it in my face when there's a potential suicide needing a shoulder to cry on. I'm still a woman when I have to go into some stinking shooting-gallery and cut out the hopped-up girls. When some drunken hooker has to be quietened down and searched you still call me, despite the fact that I'm only a woman.'

'This's different, Alice,' McCall objected. 'You and Tom were kin.'

'So?' she challenged. 'Can any of you *truthfully* claim he can go out of here and handle this case as impersonally as if the victim was a stranger?' Again the men did not reply. 'None of us can say that,' she continued. 'I know Uncle Tom was kin. But does that make me any less competent to handle the investigation?'

Still none of the men answered. Every heated word she spoke had truth in it. Alice had had four years practical detective work before she joined the office. An intelligent and able young woman, she knew investigation procedure and could not be faulted on her personal courage. For six months she worked undercover to help smash a narcotics ring, living in deadly peril every second of the time. Only male ego stood in the path of allowing her to take the case.

Jack swung his eyes from Alice to Brad, for the young deputy could claim a say in his choice of partners. For his part Brad studied Alice, reading quiet determination on her face. If they worked together Alice could, by virtue of her superior experience, be of great help; but she might also wish to take over the team as its senior member.

'Where do we start, Alice?' he asked.

Something like a low sigh left Alice's lips. Jack Tragg nodded his head, it appeared he for one agreed with Brad's decision. Before anybody could make further comment, or Alice managed to answer Brad's question, a telephone buzzed. Being nearest to it, Rafferty scooped up the receiver.

'It's D.M.V.,' he said, turning his face towards Alice and Brad. 'They made the Plymouth. Owned by James L. Greer of two-eighty-one Dorcas Crescent, Lasher Division. There was another Plymouth Fury on their stolen car list, but it was a two-tone green and white, not dark blue.'

'Tell them thanks, Pat,' Alice replied. 'We'd best check it out, Brad—— Don't you think?'

The last three words clearly came as an after-thought.

'Sure, Alice,' Brad replied. 'Does the name mean anything to anybody?'

'We could run a check on our files,' Jack suggested when nobody claimed knowledge of James L. Greer. 'But it'll be quicker for you to run across town and see him. Do you want any help along?'

Once again Alice spoke. 'There's only a slight chance of him being our man. We could have a local R.P. on hand though—— If that's all right with you, Brad.'

'Sure,' Brad confirmed. 'I'll take a corn-sheller along, might need it.'

'Go get one,' Jack ordered, showing no surprise at Brad's suggestion that he took a riot gun with him. 'I don't want a gun battle, if you can help it.'

Which might appear something of a contradiction, yet order and statement merged together rather than clashing. A Rockabye County lawman always carried a gun, so it might strike some people as strange that a deputy asked to take an extra weapon along when he went to investigate what could amount to no more than a stolen car which had not yet been missed by its innocent owner. In fact the suggestion might be thought merely ostentatious. Yet it was not. Taking the riot gun was correct and sensible peace officer tactics. Even in the hands of a master like Brad, a handgun was a weapon of limited range and power. While one could be easily and inconspicuously carried, brought into action very fast in skilled hands and provided a readily accessible *defensive* weapon, a peace officer knowing he might soon be taking the offensive preferred to have something with greater range and power on hand.

If Greer had been involved in Tom's killing, and proved to be at home when the law arrived, he would be unlikely to mildly surrender. While the psychological effect of a sudden confrontation by Brad's big automatic might be great, the sight of the riot gun's yawning .729 barrel would prove even more so. Another point to bear in mind was that Tom's killer may have used a pump-action shotgun. The Winchester Model '17 twelve gauge riot gun Brad intended to take with him cancelled the superiority of the killer's weapon over his automatic and Alice's Cobra.

Crossing the room, Brad lifted the lid of one of the boxes which flanked the door to the watch commander's office. Inside the boxes, instead of upon the traditional wall-rack, lay the office's assault armament; Thompson submachine-guns, M.1. carbines, Winchester riot guns, a telescope-sighted, bolt action rifle, ammunition for each type of weapon and two cased Federal 235 Emergency kits containing a 37-mm Gas Gun and a variety of tear-gas bombs and projectiles. He took out the riot gun which was his special charge and dropped a box of buckshot shells into his pocket. Turning, Brad walked back to Alice's side as she took her coat from the rack by the main doors to the squadroom. After helping Alice don her coat, Brad followed her from the room.

'Reckon we did right, letting them take it, Jack?' asked McCall.

'They'll handle their end,' Jack replied and glanced around the room. 'All right, boys, let's get the show on the road.'

Without needing to be told what to do, the remaining deputies started to work on different aspects of the investigation. None of them really expected the D.M.V.'s information to bring results. Even if it did, they would not regret the time spent in opening other channels.

'I'll start to shake through our files,' Larsen said. He was an enormous man, six foot five in his bare feet and two hundred and forty pounds of hard muscle; yet his voice sounded mild as a servile store clerk's when dealing with a customer.

'Go to it, Lars,' answered Valenca, taking up a telephone and dialling a number. 'Sheriff's office here. Go into the Stats. Office and start making a list of all local high-powers who use shotguns; and we'll want the record cards of all the cases Tom Cord worked on in the past—say three years for a starter.'

Normally the Records and Information Bureau, to whom Valenca spoke, would have bitched about lack of personnel on receiving such a call late Sunday night, or complained that no Statistics Office clerk was present, but not when their assistance might give a lead to a fellow officer's killer.

'Shall I call I.C.R., Jack?' asked Alvarez.

'Not until we know a bit more.'

The Identification and Criminal Records Division of the Texas Department of Public Safety in Austin acted as a gathering and holding point for crime reports for the whole state, but Jack had no wish to waste their time until he could make a request for definite information.

While Valenca and Larsen began checking for possible motives and suspects, the other two teams of Tom's watch took to the streets, prowling around, visiting informers, searching for some clue. All over the city police and deputies sought in vain, hoping to find something to help the investigation. Yet they found nothing.

In the office, deputies read through the reports of Tom's old cases as they came up out of the Stats. Office, brought along by a patrolman who for once made no complaint about his repeated trips. Time dragged by, normal departmental work carried on, yet at the back of every deputies' mind lay the thought of what he, or she, might do to help Brad and Alice.

No word came from the two deputies and about forty-five minutes after they left, Sam Cuchilo held up a data card.

'I've a hot one here, Jack,' he said, his Indian face showing animation.

Taking the card, Jack read it and nodded. 'Take it up to Central Control and put it out, Sam. I'm going to get changed, they might need some help on this one.'

CHAPTER FIVE

NEITHER Brad nor Alice spoke much as they rode the elevator to the ground floor. At the rear of the building they collected the Oldsmobile Super 88 deputy car always used by Tom and Brad. Taking the wheel, Brad let Alice ride shotgun and steered the car from its place in the geometrical pattern of assorted official vehicles which filled the lot.

Twice during the ride across town Alice opened her mouth to say something, then closed it again. She checked the car out with Central Control and then relapsed into silence. Brad let her stew in her own thoughts, thinking of the ways when Tom rode at his side and made dire threats of what he would do if Brad's driving killed them both before his approaching retirement date.

'Gordon Street,' Alice remarked and took up the transmission microphone. 'Unit SO 12 calling Cen-Con.'

'Cen-Con by!' replied the dispatcher at Central Control.

'Approaching Dorcas Crescent along Gordon. Is there an R.P. car in the vicinity?'

'R.P. 197 dispatched to rendezvous with you.'

'It's there, Alice,' Brad remarked as he swung the Oldsmobile around a curve and saw a radio patrol car waiting.

'R.P. 197 in position, Cen-Con,' Alice confirmed. 'Over and out.'

'I'm pleased that they waited here for us, instead of driving up to the front of the house,' Alice said as she hung up the microphone. Again she seemed to be on the verge of saying something more, but they drew alongside the waiting R.P. and halted before she made up her mind.

While Brad parked their car, Alice stepped out and walked towards the two patrolmen. Taking out her ID wallet, she flashed its contents.

'Deputy Fayde. That's my partner, Deputy Counter.'

She could hardly fail to notice the thinly hid relief which the R.P.'s crew showed when Brad, an obvious male deputy, swung from SO 12. Knowing that they were involved in the death of a lawman, neither cared for the idea of going to interview a possible suspect accompanied only by female deputies; no matter how cool and efficient the red head looked.

'We held the heap out here,' the older patrolman told Alice. 'I walked along the Crescent like I was foot-pounding a beat. Downstairs lights were out, the one in the upper floor went out just as I passed.'

'What do you know about Greer?' Alice asked.

'Nothing personally,' the patrolman replied. 'Records down at the House ran a check on him. Apart from minor traffic violations he's clean. A junior exec. at Sou-Tex Plastics. Married, no kids.'

'Let's go pay him a visit,' Alice ordered.

'Reckon I'll leave the corn-sheller in the heap, Alice,' Brad put in. 'I reckon this one's going to pan out empty.'

'So do I,' she admitted.

Dorcas Crescent lay off Gordon Street, being a later and slightly more expensive development. Both areas might be termed middle class, but Dorcas Crescent catered for a higher income bracket than the street. While in no way crescent-shaped, the newer development still carried the name as sounding more exclusive than a mere street. Such things mattered to the people who lived on Dorcas Crescent. The houses varied from four to eight bedroom jobs, standing in their own grounds with either a lawn or flower garden in front and patio, tennis court or small swimming pool out back. A two-car garage was a must, even if the family only owned one vehicle. The extra space indicated that the house's owner was on his way up and would soon achieve two-car family status.

On reaching 281, a four bedroomed job with all the fittings and in darkness, Alice led the way to the front door. Despite their belief that the lead would prove a dud, Alice opened her shoulder bag and the men removed the retaining straps from their guns. Precautions cost nothing and kept the one who took them alive.

Alice and one patrolman went to the right of the door, Brad and the other moving to the left. Neither pair stood before the door, but ranged alongside the wall. Reaching around, Alice thumbed the bell-push. Inside the house, a set of chimes raised a racket; that figured, a house on Dorcas Crescent would have a set of chimes instead of a lowly buzzer.

Although the chimes made a considerable noise, nothing happened for some three minutes. Then they heard it! A gentle thud at the rear of the building, as if somebody made a goof while stealthily closing a door. An instant later the listening party heard a low, muffled yelp of pain from the back of the house.

'I'll take it, Alice!' Brad snapped, and even as he spoke the automatic came into his hand.

Brad beat the others to it by a good quarter of a second, although neither patrolman could be termed slow and Alice fetched out her Cobra with surprising speed.

With one of the patrolmen on his heels, Brad sprinted along the front of the house. Light glowed in a bedroom window, but he left the dealing with that to Alice and the other man. Rounding the corner, Brad made a fast but cautious way along the side of the building, keeping to the grass verge of the rough concrete path. At the rear of the house was a large patio surrounded by a high wooden fence. Brad ignored the sun-furniture and barbecue pit which graced the patio, his full attention being reserved for the man who tried to open the fence's gate.

The patrolman held an electric torch in his left hand, keeping it extended shoulder high and at arm's length from his body as he directed the beam at the gate. Framed in the light, a tall, slim young man dropped the coat, shoes and socks he carried, but did not halt his attempt to open the gate.

'Police officers here!' Brad snapped in a clear voice which left no chance of doubt in the hearer's mind. 'Turn around slowly.'

Although the man released the handle of the gate, he neither turned nor showed any sign of relief at hearing peace officers stood behind him. From his appearance, he had good cause for the agitation he showed. His shirt's tail stuck hit-and-miss into his pants, his hair was untidy and his feet bare. The patio's surface felt rough and jagged, which probably accounted for the yelp of pain which attracted the law's attention. A man could not move bare-foot upon such a surface with impunity, nor would he without good cause. Of course the man's state of undress gave a hint that he had a good reason for taking a hurried departure—but did it also mean he possessed a guilty secret?

'G–get that light off me!' the man yelped, still not turning. 'Somebody might see me!'

'Yes, sir,' Brad agreed, 'somebody might at that. Lean forward against the gate, assume the posture!'

'D–do you know who I am?' asked the man, without obeying Brad's order.

'Mr Greer lives here. I assume you're him.'

Actually Brad assumed no such thing, but did not express his view.

'I'm Tony Vassel!' squeaked the man in a tone which suggested that the mere mention of his name should satisfy the law of his *bona fides*.

'Yes, sir?' Brad answered, sounding as if he had never heard of Tony Vassel and did not give a damn who the other might be.

Brad's attitude was only half correct. While he did not give a damn for the other man's social position, he knew full well who Tony Vassel was. Vassel worked as reporter, literary, theatrical and cinema critic for the *Gusher City Mirror*. Although the *Mirror* was a liberal-intellectual tabloid and Vassel one of it's 'brighter' employees, the young man's appearance and attitude said he could not assert his superiority over the humble peace officers behind him.

'You don't know——' Vassel began.

'And you don't appear to realise how serious your position is, Mr Vassel,' Brad interrupted. 'Make with the hands. This's the last time I'm saying it.'

At that moment a light appeared in the upper window of the neighbouring house. Vassel let out a strangled croak and hurriedly assumed the posture, placing the palms of his hands against the gate, spreading his feet apart and leaning forward. Coming up behind the reporter, Brad reached around and made a quick, but thorough hand-search for weapons. All he learned was that Vassel had not even taken the time to fasten his shirt before fleeing from the house.

'Douse the light,' Brad ordered. 'He's clean.'

'You won't get away with this!' hissed Vassel as the torch's beam flicked out.

'We haven't done anything to get away with,' Brad reminded him.

Before Vassel could start to threaten the officers with the full might and wrath of the *Mirror*, a head appeared at the lighted window next door.

'Who-all's down there?' asked a deep, masculine voice.

'The law, sir,' Brad called back. 'Everything's under control, go back to bed, please.'

'Sure, unless you need help,' came the reply, and the head disappeared.

'I'll have you before the County Commissioners' Disciplinary Board for this!' Vassel spat out.

'That's your privilege,' Brad told him calmly. 'Say, won't the *Lightning* have a ball with the story though?'

'How do you mean?' asked Vassel sullenly.

'Prowler caught escaping from house proves to be the *Mirror's* star newshawk, in a state of undress.'

A low, strangled chuckle from the patrolman followed Brad's words. Apparently the cop appreciated the situation and knew that the *Daily Lightning*, the other local newspaper, would enjoy printing a story on the lines Brad suggested. Clearly Vassel caught the point of the remark too, but he tried to bluff his way out.

'Y–you couldn't make it stick.'

'Stay right where you are!' Brad barked as the reporter began to move. 'Officer, go fetch that gent next door and ask him to step out here.'

Knowing he could never dress before the neighbour arrived and witnessed his lack of clothing, Vassel changed his tune.

'W–wait a minute. There's a simple explanation for all this.'

'Let's go around the front of the house and hear it then,' Brad ordered. 'Pick your clothes up, but don't put them on.'

While Brad headed for the disturbance at the rear, Alice prepared to handle things out front. The lit window's sash creaked as it lifted and a shape leaned out.

'Who—Who is it?' called a feminine voice.

'Police!' Alice answered, but both she and the patrolman stayed out of the patch of light thrown by the window. 'Come down and open the door, please.'

For a moment there was silence, but when the woman spoke again Alice thought she detected a note of relief in the voice.

'I can't see you.'

Alice was about to step into the light and identify herself when the patrolman caught her arm and held her back.

'Let me, ma'am.'

At another time Alice might have objected to a man taking a risk when it should fall on her, as senior officer present, to do so. However, she knew better than start debating women's right to equal chances and duties at that moment.

'Go ahead,' she answered and hefted the Cobra. 'I'll cover you—and I shoot "Expert".'

'Now that's a real comforting thought,' grinned the man.

For all the levity in his tone, the patrolman advanced into the light with all the caution of a whitetail deer crossing a clearing in well-hunted country. He was prepared to make a flying dive for cover if the shape in the window made a hostile move, or should a second figure appear. Looking up, he saw only a pretty young woman with untidy blonde hair and wearing a quilted robe. Nothing happened to make him regret breaking a life-time rule of never volunteering for a task a senior officer should perform.

'What do you want?' asked the woman in the window, satisfied that a genuine Gusher City patrolman stood below.

Holstering her Cobra as she stepped into the light, Alice replied, 'Come down and open the door, please. We don't want to disturb the neighbours, Mrs Greer.'

Mrs Greer appeared to share Alice's wish to avoid disturbing her neighbours, although probably for less altruistic reasons. Pulling in her head, she disappeared from sight. A few seconds later the hall lights came on and bare feet padded across the floor to the front door. Opening the front door on its chain, the woman peered out, studied Alice's open ID wallet, then unfastened the chain and stood back.

'Come in. What do you want?'

Still with her hand on the Cobra's butt, even though the gun lay hidden in her bag, Alice entered the hall. She saw nothing to arouse her suspicions. The woman proved to be Alice's height, shapely; and nervous, if the glances she directed at the rear of the building be anything to go on. From glimpses Alice got through the front of the robe, Mrs Greer either wore a very brief shortie nightdress, or nothing, underneath.

'I don't underst——' the woman began, then a look of shock came to her face as she stared past Alice to where Vassel came into sight followed by Brad. 'Tony!' she shrieked. 'You said you could——'

'Shut up!' Vassel spat out, gaining courage now he was out of sight of independent witnesses. 'They can't hang a 502 rap on us.'

Instead of shutting up, Mrs Greer let out another shriek, this time one of anger, for she did not know the various articles of the Texas Penal Code and drew her own conclusion what Article 502 covered. Like many law-abiding citizens, she assumed that women officers handled only three types of work, juvenile delinquency, traffic—and prostitution. Being too old to class as a juvenile delinquent, knowing the police would never arrive at that hour and in such numbers merely to query a traffic violation, only one alternative remained. Mrs Greer did not care to think about that alternative.

'How dare you?' she screeched, facing Alice like a hound-treed alley-cat. 'Do I look like a pros—— Ooh! Just wait until my husb——'

For a second time in her angry tirade Mrs Greer chopped short her words. A well-mannered lady did not ask people, even peace officers, if she looked like a prostitute; and, in view of the circumstances, she could hardly threaten the visitors with her husband's righteous, tax-paying wrath.

'We never mentioned prostitution, Mrs Greer,' Alice pointed out. 'Article 502 of the Texas Penal Code covers adultery; which means voluntary sexual intercourse between a married person and a person other than the offender's wife or husband. We have made no mention of that, either.'

'Don't worry, Vi,' Vassel put in. 'Article 502's void these days.'

'Mister,' Brad drawled. 'I'd hate like hell to depend on a

judge thinking the same way.'

'You've no right to censure our morals,' Vassel stated, more in a whine than with his usual condescending manner when addressing a peace officer.

'Nor wish to,' snapped Alice. 'Is he clean, Brad?'

'We don't want him for anything,' Brad replied.

'Then I'd suggest you dress and leave.'

'You—you don't want me?' gasped Vassel, relief plain in his voice.

'Not even gift-wrapped and with a brand-new Cadillac to boot,' Brad answered, jerking a contemptuous thumb towards the door. 'Screw.'

With all the courage and stand-fast spirit of a rat deserting a sinking ship, Vassel turned and darted from the room, not even waiting to do more than slip on his shoes.

Finding herself deserted, Mrs Greer let out a wail. Her indignation had gone in the face of knowing what offence Article 502 covered. Such a charge, if made, would damage her socially far more than an accusation of prostitution—which was easily disproved and which nobody would believe of her. Alice studied the crying woman and made a sign which sent Brad and the two policemen from the house. Left alone with Mrs Greer, and seeing the woman to be in a state verging on a suicide attempt, Alice soothed her before talking about the business which had brought the law to 281 Dorcas Crescent.

Punctuated by sniffs and tears, Mrs Greer's story came out. Apparently her husband insisted on taking their only car when he went to El Paso on business, causing a quarrel just before his departure. Then, although he left on Friday afternoon, he did not call his wife until late Saturday which did nothing to heal the breach. Still angry, Mrs Greer had accepted an invitation to a party on Sunday night. She took a couple of drinks too many, met Vassel and before she had realised quite what was happening found herself at home, in bed with the reporter. On hearing the door's chimes, they assumed it to be her husband returned unexpectedly. Vassel seemed to have experience in such situations, for he grabbed his clothes and told her to stall for a short time while he slipped out of the rear door.

Now Mrs Greer wished she was dead.

Not wanting to spend the night coping with a potential suicide, Alice suggested a way out of Mrs Greer's difficulties. The neighbours would talk and Greer was certain to learn about the visit by the law. So Alice promised to arrange that the local station house claimed to have sent a car to investigate a prowler call and found a man, somewhat drunk but otherwise innocent, had taken the wrong turning on his way home and blundered into the Greer's patio. The story left Mrs Greer in the clear, with only her conscience to bother her. However, it served Alice's purpose in calming the woman down.

While Alice believed Mrs Greer's story, she was a trained peace officer and, as such, like the fabled character from Missouri, must be shown. On leaving the house, she found that Brad had checked out the garage, found it empty and dismissed the patrolmen. While walking back to their car, Alice filled Brad in on what she knew and said they would check with the El Paso law to make sure Greer was in town.

Once more Brad took the wheel of the car and Alice called in her report to Cen-Con. Her message arrived just as Sam Cuchilo entered the radio room.

'Alice, Brad,' he said, taking the microphone from the dispatcher. 'We've a hot one for you. Floyd Goole. Tom put him away on a three-stretch for slow-elking.[1] Goole made some threats at his trial. He's been out for about three months—and he always used a pump-action shotgun for butchering the stolen cattle.'

[1] *Slow-elking: Illegally killing and butchering stolen cattle.*

CHAPTER SIX

ALICE and Brad exchanged glances as they heard Cuchilo's message.

'Where do we find him, Sam?' she asked.

'Runs a cap-and-ball spread about three miles past Hoseville, lies about a mile back off the right of the State Auto Road.'

Again the exchange of glances and Brad nodded to answer the girl's unasked question.

'Brad and I'll go and check him out, Sam,' Alice announced.

'Tonight?'

'Can you think of a better time?'

'All right, Alice. I'll call Buck Shields in Hoseville and ask him to join the party.'

'Do that. Tell him to bring tea and fancy cakes. Over and out.'

Even while Alice spoke, Brad had been steering the car towards the edge of town. Once clear of the city limits and on the State Auto Road, he built up the Oldsmobile's speed to keep the speedometer needle flickering beyond the seventy mark. Due to it being Sunday, the road carried little traffic and so Brad did not use the siren, although the red light flashed on the vehicle's roof.

'Cen-Con to SO 12!' The radio crackled alive before they had covered half of the thirty mile run to Hoseville.

'SO 12 by!' Alice replied.

'Bad news, Alice,' it was Sam Cuchilo speaking. 'Buck's crew are out on the road-block and covering back-country trails. Jack doesn't want to pull any of them in so he's flying up to join you with the chopper. Wait for him before you move in. "Code One"?'

'Roger and out.'

'Code One' meant acknowledge message and Alice's reply told Cuchilo she both heard and understood. Her eyes dropped to the riot gun in the clamps at the side of her seat. The weapon had not been needed at Dorcas Crescent, but might still be required.

The car sped along a road built for handling fast-moving traffic and Alice sat watching the open range drop behind them. Knowing Brad needed to concentrate on handling the Oldsmobile, she did not speak. She thought, however, and the nagging worry which had followed her since being accepted on the assignment returned. By the time the Hoseville turn-off had been passed, Alice came to a decision. The issue must be faced and settled, there was no point in putting it off any longer.

Ahead lay a signpost pointing along a dirt trail and announcing 'F. GOOLE'. Sucking in her breath, she spoke and made the words come out as a direct order for the first time.

'This's it, Brad. Kill the lights and hold the noise down.'

'You're getting real bossy, ma'am,' Brad replied, slowing the car.

'I'm sorry, Brad, but——'

'What is it John Wayne says?' Brad interrupted. 'Something about never apologising, it being a sign of weakness.' He stopped the car but made no move to climb out and open the gate. Instead he turned to look at the slightly defiant girl and a smile flickered on his lips. 'We may as well thrash this thing out right now. One of us has to be boss of the team. Well, I'm taller and heavier than you, got bigger muscles—and a better gun.' Even at such a moment Brad could not forget that he was an automatic pistol fan in the presence of somebody foolish enough to carry a revolver. 'Got more hair on my chest if it comes to that. But on this case none of that counts. What's needed to be boss is experience—and lady, you've got the experience!'

A sudden suspicion hit Alice and she glared at Brad. 'You've known all along what's been bugging me.'

'Why sure.'

'And what did your little speech mean?'

'That as far as I've been concerned all along, you're the boss.'

Slowly Alice let out her breath in a long sigh. She had known the subject of who ran the team must arise sooner or later and feared the moment when it came, not being sure of how the big male deputy would react to the idea of taking orders from a woman. Now she knew; and figured they could function more smoothly as a team for knowing.

'You might not like me being boss,' she warned.

'Psychiatrists do say we all subconsciously hate our bosses,' Brad answered. 'I'll try to hide it.'

A thought struck Alice as her partner left the car and opened the gate to allow them access to Goole's property. When Brad returned to the car, she raised the matter.

'Say, how do you know you've more hair on your chest than I have?'

'I saw you wearing a bikini at the Lakeside Club's pool,' Brad explained. 'They'd've been mighty slim hairs to hide under it. Mind though, I'm always willing to show for most.'

'I've heard all about you Counters,' Alice stated. 'Read Mark's book of memoirs when your folks brought it out.'

'Drat Great-Grandpappy Mark,' grinned Brad, starting the car and driving through the gate. 'He plumb ruined the family's reputation—I'm pleased to say.'

The car rolled along the track, but inside the slight air of tension had departed. After covering a mile or so across the open range, with the car's lights out and the engine making a barely audible purr, they topped a ridge and saw the Goole place below. Brad stopped the car and they surveyed the situation. Lights glowed at the windows of the small, one-storey, frame house, showing a large truck parked before it. A few horses milled in the corral to the left of the buildings and on the right, also lit up, stood a barn, its doors open. Even as they watched, Brad and Alice saw a man pass before the open doorway on the inside of the barn.

'Unit SO 12 to Cen-Con!' Alice said into the microphone as Brad reversed the car. 'In position over-looking Goole ranch. Where is support?'

'Sheriff delayed, has only just reached landing strip,' Cuchilo replied.

'There's some activity at the house,' Alice went on. 'Is Goole the kind of man who'd pay his hired help double time for working this late on a Sunday?'

'He's tighter than a duck's butt and that's water-tight,' Cuchilo answered. 'Sorry, Alice.'

'So you should be, using such expressions to a lady,' she smiled, it had been many years since such a comment raised a blush on her cheeks. Then she stopped smiling and made a decision. 'Brad and I'll have to move in, Sam. If Goole's up to something, he'll hole up and paint for war the moment he hears the chopper.'

'Good luck. May *Ka-Dih* guide your steps, white-eye sister. I'll inform Jack. Over and out.'

'Nice to know we have the Comanche Great Spirit on our side,' Brad remarked as he took up his riot gun and opened the car's door.

'Comforting,' Alice agreed. 'I only hope *Ka-Dih* heard Sam's request. Wonder what they're doing down there?'

'Now me,' said Brad, holding his voice down. 'I'm more interested in whether he keeps any dogs around the place.'

'We'll soon know the answer to both. Let's go.'

'Wouldn't want to borrow a *gun*, would you?'

'This's no time to start a firearms argument,' smiled Alice. 'Leave us try to keep the blind side of the barn between us and the house.'

While moving down the slope, Alice marvelled at the light-footed manner in which Brad glided over the ground. For all his size and build, he moved lightly on his feet. Keeping alert and stepping cautiously, they advanced down the slope. Alice blessed the inspiration which led her to go home and change into slacks before reporting to the office. A cocktail gown, sheer nylons and spike-heels were definitely not the thing for such an occasion.

'No dogs!' Brad breathed in relief as they reached the side of the barn. 'They'd've heard us for sure, and started bawling, if there had been.'

Cautiously he peered around the corner of the barn, but saw no sign of life on the front of the house. Followed by Alice, who held her Cobra, and with his riot gun gripped in the ready position, Brad advanced silently along the front of the barn. From inside came a dull smacking sound such as one occasionally hears in a butcher's shop.

On stepping through the open barn doors, the deputies answered their second question, what Goole was doing at that hour of a Sunday night. Standing with his back to them, a big, burly, crop-haired man in his shirt sleeves wearing a butcher's apron, used a meat cleaver on a side of freshly killed beef.

'Mr Goole?' Brad said quietly.

Instantly the man turned, starting to raise the cleaver in a threatening manner. Then he froze as the yawning bore of the riot gun lined squarely on him. He scowled at Brad, who still wore his shooting clothes but had pinned on his deputy's badge, and from Brad turned his eyes to Alice, recognising the uniform of a woman deputy.

'Who're you?' he growled, more to gain time than through necessity.

'Deputies out of the sheriff's office,' Brad replied, moving forward slowly with Alice on his heels. 'Drop the cleaver and step this way.'

'Are you Mr Goole?' Alice went on as the man sullenly tossed his cleaver into a corner of the barn, where it landed on a rolled-up cow hide.

'Yeah!' came the surly reply.

'Where've you been all night?' Brad snapped.

'Picking daisies,' Goole answered, throwing a sullen glance at the hide.

'Don't crack wise, *hombre*!' warned Brad. 'I said——'

'Hey, Floyd!' yelled a voice from outside. 'How much longer you going to be?'

Only for an instant did Brad take his eyes from Goole, but it proved long enough. Showing remarkable speed for so bulky a man—Goole stood as tall as Brad and weighed heavier—the rancher sprang forward. His big, blood-stained hands deflected and clamped hold of the riot gun, trying to wrest the weapon from Brad's grasp. At the same moment Goole let out a bellow for help and feet thudded outside the barn as men ran to his assistance.

Alice threw a quick glance at where the two big men struggled for possession of the gun. Having seen Brad in action at the gym, and on duty, she figured he stood a better than fair chance of handling Goole, so she gave her full attention to dealing with the rescue party.

Flattening herself at the side of the door, Alice waited. She timed her opening move just right. As the first man, a tall gangling cowhand, burst through the doorway, she thrust out her leg. Unable to stop, the man tripped over Alice's leg and went sprawling to the floor. In this he came off lighter than the second of his party. Wearing a peaked baseball cap, wind-cheater and jeans, the second man made his entrance carrying an open switch-blade knife. Seeing the weapon, Alice lashed her right arm around in a backhand swing that drove the butt of the Cobra under the man's chin and full into his adam's apple. Letting out a strangled croak and dropping his knife, the man stumbled back into the arms of the third member of the party.

The third man showed speed and a keen judgement of the situation. Shoving the second rescuer, the third sent him staggering towards Alice and reached under his denim jacket, stepping forward. He came to a halt as the girl avoided his path and came into view. While the third man had read fire-arms magazines and believed articles on the subject of the .38 Special's lack of stopping power, he reckoned such a bullet would severely damage him at the distance from which Alice covered him.

'Hit the wall!' she snapped, moving to cover all three and still be able to lend a hand should Brad need one.

When Goole jumped Brad, he expected a comparatively easy time. Taking Brad's upper-crust Southern drawl along with the expensive clothing, Goole figured the blond to be a rich sport taken on as an honorary officer to keep his family happy. So the rancher expected little trouble in gaining possession of the riot gun. He found himself tangling with a man even stronger than himself.

Bracing their feet apart, the two men exerted their strength in the effort each made to free the gun from the other's grasp. Gasping slightly, sweat trickling down his face, Goole staked everything on driving up a knee in an attempt to catch Brad's groin and force an immediate release, or a weakening of the deputy's grip. Brad had learned roughhouse fighting from cowhands and oil-field workers, in addition to gaining a thorough knowledge of boxing, savate, karate and judo. Twisting his lower body without loosening his grip, he took the knee on his hip. Then he gave a tremendous surging heave. Caught off balance, Goole felt his feet leave the floor. He lost his hold on the gun in his amazement and staggered back. Not quite far enough. Like a flash, Brad brought around the gun, driving its butt against the side of Goole's jaw. The force of the blow, taken with catching him off balance, pitched Goole bodily across the room. The whole building rocked as he smashed into the wall and when he slid down, he lay without a move.

Brad whirled around, slanting the Winchester hip high in the direction of the door, but found Alice had the situation well in hand.

'You had to do it the hard way,' she remarked.

Before Brad could think up a suitable comment, he heard the rotor beats of a helicopter approaching.

'Freeze, boys!' he ordered, seeing the three rescuers tense. 'Go out and put down the red carpet, boss lady.'

'Don't let them take your gun while I'm gone,' she replied.

Despite his grin at the girl's words, Brad stayed alert and kept his attention on the trio of prisoners. While they knew the helicopter brought reinforcements for the law, not one tried to make a break. Against a man holding a handgun they might have chanced a dash for freedom; but not when covered by a riot gun. Buckshot spread and would not miss at such close range; a skilled man could work the pump-action of a Winchester Model '17 almost as fast as a semi-automatic weapon's mechanism churned lead out. Brad's decision to fetch along the riot gun was justified in that it prevented further trouble.

Jack Tragg had taken time out to change into his uniform and carried a stag-horn butted Colt Single Action Army revolver—a modern version of the fabulous old Peacemaker traditionally used by every great old-time gun fighter—thrust into his waistband; an M.1. carbine dangling in his right hand. The uniform and revolver were spares he kept at the office, but he did not have a reserve belt. A man who wanted to stay alive did not borrow a gunbelt when going into what might be a fight.

Followed by Alice, Larsen and Valenca, who had flown up in the helicopter with the sheriff, Jack entered the barn and took in the scene. From the butchered beef, his eyes went to a groaning Goole as the rancher tried to get to his feet.

'Well, well, well,' Jack said. 'You've been slow-elking again, Floyd.'

Rubbing his jaw, Goole turned and sat with his back against the wall. 'It's the first time since I came out. Who stooled on me?'

'Where were you at nine-fifty last night?' Brad asked, walking towards Goole at the sheriff's side.

'Here, where else?'

'How about outside the depot on Station Street?'

'Why in hell should I be there?'

'To kill Tom Cord,' Brad answered, watching the man's face.

There could be no mistaking the surprise which twisted Goole's surly features. 'To kill—— Did somebody do that?'

'Yes,' Brad said flatly.

Goole saw the big deputy tense slightly and held down the comment which rose automatically. Having received a sample of Brad's strength, Goole did not wish to receive a full portion; and he figured he might, despite the sheriff's strict orders on the subject of handling prisoners, if he took to abusing or mean-mouthing the dead deputy.

Then Goole realised why the law had descended upon him at such an inopportune moment. 'Hey!' he yelped, rising hurriedly in his agitation. 'Am I crazy or something? Do I have rocks in my head? Would I wash a badge and come back here to fix an alibi by letting you catch me slow-elking?'

'You've a point there,' the sheriff admitted. 'Where-at's your shotgun?'

'Up to the house. I don't use it no more. Got me a humane killer, it makes less noise and mess. I haven't used the Stevens in weeks.'

'I hope for your sake you're right,' Jack answered. 'Go check it out, Brad. Take Lars with you.'

'Alice's my partner,' Brad replied.

A grin creased Jack's face as he watched Alice and Brad leave the barn. A team worked as such, or failed, that meant the girl and blond went to the house together even if they might find more members of Goole's crowd inside. From the look of the barn, they could take good care of themselves.

At the house Alice wrapped her handkerchief over her palm and took down the Stevens Model 77 pump-action shotgun from its place over the fireplace. They had found the house to be deserted, although they entered ready for trouble.

'It's clean,' she stated after peeking into the barrel. 'F.I.L.'ll be able to say roughly when it was fired last.'

'Sure,' Brad agreed. 'Trouble is, Alice, I think Goole's clean.'

'So do I,' Alice admitted. 'He'd know we would be looking for him and the last thing he'd do was start making big antelope[1] tonight. He's a five to ten stretch ahead of him. No, Brad, I don't think Goole's our man.'

[1] *Big antelope: another name for illegally butchered beef.*

CHAPTER SEVEN

At about the time Alice and Brad left Headquarters Building to visit the Greer house, a frightened man was working in a garage on Jenner Street in the part of Gusher City known as The Bad-Bit. He stood by the side of a Plymouth Fury car, rapidly spraying a coat of parkway-green paint over its dark blue body. Sweat rolled down the man's face as he worked. To prevent any chance of light showing and arousing suspicions, he had covered all the windows with thick drapes and plugged the crack at the bottom of the roll-down doors.

Lowering the spray-gun for a moment, the man wiped sweat from his face. He had never expected anything like *that* when he received orders to change the Plymouth's original two-tone coloration to a dark blue finish, fit it with the licence plates provided by the man who gave him his orders and deliver it to a parking lot on the fringe of Greevers.

Sure he knew a crime would be committed in the car, but not the killing of a deputy sheriff. At the worst, he figured a safe job—either blowing it by explosives, or taking it away for leisurely opening—or maybe a window-breaking at some uptown jewellery or fur store. But a wash job: a contract with a lawman as victim, that was something entirely different. Everybody knew the law never let up when one of their own had been the victim in a murder attempt.

The man wondered what he ought to do for the best. While working for a hot-car ring, he had no criminal connections, other than the man who gave him his orders, delivered vehicles to be worked on and paid him. In fact he did not even know how to contact his sole connection with the outfit. His original orders had been to collect the car from where he left it, bring it to his garage and alter its colour after destroying the plates. Already acid ate away at the licence plates and he had begun the repainting when the news broke over the radio. Fear gnawed at him as the implication of what he heard struck him. Under his orders, he should finish painting the Fury and hold it until his contact collected and disposed of it through the outfit's channels. Now a lawman had been killed from the car, it was too hot for such handling.

There was another point eating at the man, one which worried him even more than the possession of a red-hot car. Arriving early at the rendezvous, he had seen the two men drive up, even spoke to them as they left the car. Men who gunned down a badge did not take kindly to the thought of being recognised. However, if he knew anything of the organisation behind the killers, they ought to be long gone from Gusher City by now.

A low buzzing sound came to the man's ears. He swung around, face working nervously, for he had not been expecting anybody to come to his side door at that hour of a Sunday evening. Again the buzzer sounded, a long, angry blast. Clearly the caller intended to be admitted and the owner had no wish for a disturbance that might attract a beat patrolman's attention. Crossing the room, he switched out the lights and stepped into the passage which separated the workshop from his living-quarters. He walked along the passage towards the door opening on to the alley alongside the building.

'You!' he gasped, staring at the two shapes which confronted him as he opened the door.

'Us,' agreed Jordan, stepping into the building with Sleath on his heels. 'You was expecting maybe Adam Flint and Frank Arcaro?'

'Wh-what do you want?' the garage-owner asked; for while he had not expected to see the detectives of the *Naked City* television show, he also did not expect to come face to face with the two killers again.

'Come to see you, buddy-buddy,' Sleath answered in his high-pitched voice. 'This town's jumping with law. They're searching luggage at the airport already.'

'L-look, fellers,' croaked the owner. 'I'm clear here. The law don't make me part of the mob. I don't know if the top men would go for me hiding you.'

Between them the killers backed the owner along the passage and into his workshop. Sleath clicked on the lights and they gave the room a searching study, with particular attention to the half-painted Plymouth.

The patrolman's guess at the killers' appearance had been good. Both topped the six foot mark, Jordan just making it and Sleath two inches above it. Now they wore lightweight topcoats, but each retained his dark-coloured fedora hat. Under the coats Jordan wore a navy blue business suit, while Sleath's was dark brown. In appearance the two men were very different. Jordan had wide shoulders and the tanned jovial face of an outdoors man. Slimmer and pallid-featured, Sleath looked a city dweller. Normally his face bore an expression of pious, slightly hypocritical, self-effacement. In his home town he was known as a pillar of the church, a do-gooder always ready to champion the cause of banning something or other that most people enjoyed doing. One could not imagine two such opposite types of men, Jordan the breezy extrovert and Sleath the reverse, working together; a valuable asset in their trade.

'The cops are jumping, pally,' Jordan remarked, setting down a grip and a case of the type used by sportsmen to transport firearms. 'Tie that for us.'

'I don't dig you,' answered the owner, flicking nervous glances first at Sleath then back to Jordan.

'At the airport, buddy-buddy,' Sleath put in, placing his suitcase upon a work bench. 'That hack driver who picked us up was real hip. He drove by instead of pulling straight in. The law stopped two guys carrying gun-cases as we passed. Now that's moving, man, to be covering the airport so quickly.'

Somehow Sleath scared the garage-owner far more than did Jordan. One did not expect such a man to be a cold-blooded professional killer.

'They always jump when a badge's been killed,' the owner said.

Sleath and Jordan exchanged glances.

'I told you so,' Sleath announced, almost with satisfaction. 'Just like that Chicago contract.'

'You told me,' agreed Jordan. 'Thing is, what do we do now?'

'We make a call to the man, that's what we do. You stay here and keep buddy-buddy company. He looks like he needs company, just so he don't feel lonesome and neglected.'

'Yeah. He looks that way.'

Time dragged by. Twice the owner picked up his spray-gun and set it down, aware all the time that Jordan's eyes never left him. At last the man felt he must say something.

'This heap's hot,' he got out. 'Too hot now. The mob won't dare move a Fury for months.'

'Won't, huh?' grunted Jordan.

'I should take it out and dump it.'

'Should, huh?'

'S-sure.'

At that moment Sleath returned from making his telephone call in the rear of the building. Leaning on the work-bench with a hand on his case, he studied the scared face of the garage-owner.

'How'd you know it was a badge we burned, buddy-buddy?'

'There was a newsflash on the radio.'

'And now you're scared?'

Something in Sleath's voice gave the man a warning and caused him to try to put on a bold front.

'M-me! Naw! I'm not scared!'

'Not, huh?' asked Jordan.

'No, I'm not,' answered the owner, but he did not sound convincing.

'That's good, buddy-buddy,' purred Sleath, turning his back on the man and opening his case. 'A scared guy makes bad mistakes.'

'Like wanting to take this heap out of here and dump it,' Jordan went on. 'A heap that's red-hot and only half-painted. A scared guy'd want to take that heap and drive around the streets crawling with cops looking for it. A guy who's scared'd draws attention to himself and gets picked up. He might even be scared enough to talk.'

'I—I don't dig you,' whispered the owner. 'All I know is that I had to deliver this heap and collect it later.'

'You know something else, buddy-buddy,' Sleath stated, still with his back to the man and doing something in his case.

'What else?' gasped the man, growing more terrified by the

second.

'The hack-driver followed orders. He never looked at us. You did. You know what we look like.'

And with that Sleath swung to face the man, a revolver with a bulging silencer fitted to its barrel in his hand. A look of shocked terror etched itself on the man's face. He froze, standing rigid and speechless. Even as he opened his mouth to say something, he died. The revolver kicked in Sleath's hand, making only a low hiss as the silencer's baffle-plates killed the noise of the muzzle-blast. Jerking up on to his toes under the impact of the bullet—a silencer does not reduce velocity or striking power to any noticeable degree—the garage-owner spun around and fell against the side of the car. Three times more Sleath fired, sending the bullets into the man's back.

Jordan stood very still. Long experience had taught him never to make a move when Sleath handled a gun. He watched the body slide down, its fingers scrabbling at the car's side, the clothing wiping away some of the paint so recently applied.

Slowly the mask of savage pleasure left Sleath's face and he removed the gun's silencer. 'That's what the man said,' he told Jordan. 'He said wash the guy if he looked like running scared. Then we're to lay low in town until the man gives the word. He says this county's sewed up tighter than a widow's purse-strings, so we stay on here until it's safe to move.'

'That figures,' Jordan grunted. 'Did we get sold, or did somebody goof?'

'I don't know,' Sleath admitted, jerking a thumb towards the body. 'How about buddy-buddy there?'

For a moment Jordan did not reply, then he looked around the workshop and saw an answer to their problem.

'I hope cremation's not against his religious beliefs.'

'Huh?' grunted Sleath.

'I once worked as cover for a torch mob and know how to fire a joint like this so it'll burn up good.'

Sleath ran the tip of his tongue over his lips and interest sparked in his eyes. 'When do we do it?' he asked eagerly.

'What say we hide out here until morning? Then we'll set the torch and slip out. We'd be less conspicuous in daylight than prowling the streets at night.'

'Be best,' agreed Sleath and looked at the gun-case. 'You'd

best leave that scatter behind.'

Jordan nodded his head sadly. Since buying the Brushmaster, he had come to look upon it as a lucky gun. Jordan was a superstitious man: if he lost his first taker during a day's fishing, he expected to do badly; should he miss his first shot on the opening day of a bird-shooting season, he looked forward to poor results in the future. He had never run into any trouble before while using the Brushmaster and did not care to lose his lucky piece. However, he knew he could not take the gun with him. Its one defect in his line of work had finally come up. The forty-and-a-half inch length of the gun prevented it from being easily concealed and any man seen carrying a gun-case in Gusher City would surely be questioned by the law. Extra attention would be given to a man owning a gun such as the Brushmaster, designed specifically for accurate shooting with a buckshot load.

'I'll leave it in the car with this creep,' he announced. 'It's a pity though, this's a real good gun.'

'Make the man spring for a new one,' Sleath suggested. 'Douse the lights and let's get some sleep. I hope buddy-buddy there has an electric razor so I can shave before I leave in the morning.'

CHAPTER EIGHT

WISHING to form a better impression of how Alice and Brad worked as a team, Jack Tragg rode back to Gusher City in their car. He left Larsen and Valenca to hold the prisoners until a wagon arrived for them, dismissed the helicopter and took the rear seat of the Oldsmobile. Although Alice and Brad had been responsible for Goole's capture, their other case took priority; so the other team of deputies would handle the tying up of the slow-elking.

'I told Lars and Tony to go over the place with a fine-tooth comb to see if Goole has another shotgun,' Jack remarked.

'He might have, but I don't think he's involved with our case,' Alice answered and threw a glance at Brad. 'What do you think?'

'Huh?' Brad grunted, taking his eyes from the road for a moment. Clearly he had not been listening to a word.

'All right, Brad,' Jack said, knowing the blond deputy pretty well. 'Spit it out.'

'Sure,' Alice agreed. 'Something's bugging you, has been ever since we left Goole's spread.'

'No more poker games for me,' Brad sighed. then became serious. 'I've been thinking of the way Tom was killed.'

'What aspect of it?' Alice asked.

'The way the whole thing was handled. First they park their heap in just the right place——'

'Had the side of the street to pick from, being Sunday night,' Jack pointed out. 'Naturally they'd park there.'

'Sure. But they paid the parking meter so that if a cop came along he wouldn't bother them any in passing. The average punk wouldn't think of a thing like that. And I don't reckon Goole's smart enough to have thought of it either.'

'I'll buy that, Floyd's not bright,' agreed Jack. 'But how about the Fury's licence plates?'

'Maybe the patrolman made a mistake,' Alice suggested. 'It has been known to happen—even in the Bureau of Women Officers.'

'I'd have said particularly in B.W.O.,' smiled Jack. 'Only for a mistake he hit well, picking the number of another dark blue Plymouth Fury to send in.'

'Did Schuster make a mistake, Brad?' asked Alice.

'I don't think so,' Brad replied. 'I reckon that Fury was the stolen two-tone. A hot-car mob can repaint a heap and have it ready to roll in under forty-eight hours. But the killers didn't want to take any chances. They arranged for copies of a genuine set of plates from a matching car be fitted. If a cop became suspicious and called in a make, he'd learn that such a car existed in town and hadn't been reported missing.'

'Which implies local knowledge,' Alice remarked.

'Or good organisation—by professionals brought in for the job.'

For a time none of the trio spoke, then Jack asked, 'Do you buy that, Brad?'

'Maybe more than a couple of local punks with a grudge.'

'How would they know where to find Tom?' Jack went on, but not in a tone of derision.

'That we don't know,' Brad admitted. 'It was pretty common knowledge around the House that Tom went to San Antonio on business and would be back tonight, and that he went by train. Maybe somebody found out——'

'One thing's for sure,' Alice said as Brad's words trailed off. 'They were waiting and didn't make their hit on chance. It would be too much of a coincidence for them to be there, waiting, with a shotgun on hand, on the off chance.'

'Coincidences do happen,' Jack remarked.

'Sure, but—— Suppose they hit the wrong man?'

'That's not likely, Alice,' Brad objected. 'We know that Tom was the last man out of the depot. He came out alone, so they couldn't have mistaken him for anybody among the crowd.'

'We'll put it over the air and television news services that we'd like to interview passengers from the train, question the hack-drivers, see if anybody resembling Tom in height and build left the train. If there was, we'll run a check.'

'If the killers were imported professionals,' Brad said slowly, clearly thinking out his words, 'they'd have an escape route planned.'

'Not in the Fury,' Alice answered. 'They'd need to change cars and even then two men travelling together would attract attention. Professionals would know how fast we'd move when we heard one of our own had been hit. I don't think they'd chance a car.'

'Which leaves train, bus or fly out,' Jack commented. 'And they'd know we would be watching all three. Call Cen-Con, Alice, arrange to have a check made with the airport and bus depot to find out if anybody booked a trip and failed to show for it.'

'Yo!' Alice replied, and took up the transmission microphone. It was a long chance, but all they had at the moment.

On returning to the sheriff's office, Alice found an answer to her request for information. Sitting at Brad's desk, she read the sheet of paper left by the dispatch clerk who took the message.

'Negative from the bus depot,' she said. 'A Mr Sudwick cancelled reservations for himself and his wife on the ten forty-five East-bound flight. He called in to cancel at nine-thirty.'

'Which lets him out,' grunted Jack.

'Sure. But there were two more cancellations—well, not cancellations, but non-arrivals for bookings. Both bookings were male, made within fifteen minutes of each other this afternoon, or yesterday afternoon seeing that it's Monday morning. Otis B. Jackson, address given was the Newnes Hotel in Leander.'

'Know the place,' Jack interrupted. 'Respectable, middle-rent district, not a crook hang-out. How about the other.'

'Frederick Sloane. He called from the Bestwick Temperance House in Evans Hill.'

'Apart from the temperance side, the same type of place as the Newnes,' Jack breathed. 'And neither of them showed to collect their reservations?'

'That's what the paper says,' Alice replied, meeting Jack's eyes.

'It's worth checking out,' the sheriff stated. 'Go after Brad fetches up the coffee.'

As if hearing his name, Brad entered the squadroom, carrying a tray with a large pot of coffee on it, and followed by Grantley and Melnick.

'Nothing, Jack,' Grantley announced. 'We've prowled every inch of the Hardin Street area, stopped pedestrians, called at gas-stations, bars, every place, but nobody seems to have seen a dark blue Plymouth.'

'The damned thing just couldn't disappear,' Alice objected.

'You know it, I know it,' grunted Grantley, 'the trouble being that the car doesn't seem to know it.'

He knew Alice well, for she had been his wife's best friend and one-time beat partner. In fact Grantley had been one of the men who recommended Alice as the best candidate for promotion to woman deputy; and he did not do it to placate his now-retired wife.

'Once out of the immediate area, they'd slow down and drive normally,' the girl guessed. 'Who notices a car as long as it doesn't do anything unusual?'

'Not enough folks, and that's for sure,' Jack said, and took a cup from the tray Brad set on the desk. 'Brad reckons we're dealing with professionals and the hit was a well-organised contract.'

Something in the sheriff's voice drew Alice's eyes to him. Jack's tones held none of the derision usually shown when a young, inexperienced officer made a suggestion based more on sensationalism than cold facts. The words showed that Jack regarded Brad as a member of his staff whose opinions were worthy of serious condideration.

'It could be, at that,' agreed Grantley. 'Jake and me're cutting back in the morning, Jack. If there's nothing for us, we'll go hit the sack.'

'We've a lead we want running down. Could you go to the Bestwick and check out a Frederick Sloane?'

'Sure,' confirmed Grantley.

While a deputy was on call twenty-four hours a day, Jack always asked if he wanted a man to stay on beyond the end of a watch. While the end result was the same, his men liked the touch of having it come as a request.

'We'll take the Newnes,' Alice remarked, pouring a cup of coffee which Melnick appropriated. 'A temperance hotel is more in Jake and Ian's line.'

'You're just riled because you've had to pour our coffee for us,' Grantley told her, having taken the first cup she filled.

After finally gaining possession of and drinking a cup of coffee, Alice went with Brad to their car. This time she took the wheel and drove the Oldsmobile out into the sleeping city, taking the shortest route to the Newnes Hotel.

'Let's leave the heap out here,' Brad suggested as the girl brought the Oldsmobile towards the front of the hotel. 'Why bother with the parking lot?'

'There's a No-Parking sign out front,' Alice pointed out.

'We're not likely to get a ticket at this hour of the night,' Brad answered. 'Anyways, I've a five in the back of my driver's licence.'

'And you an officer of the law, duly appointed and sworn to keep the peace,' Alice smiled. 'Shame on you, Bradford Counter.'

Even though they had suffered a personal loss that night and were tired from long hours of driving and work, life must go on. It helped to make the tired old peace officer jokes.

Leaving the car parked, in defiance of the Traffic Bureau's warning sign, before the doors of the Newnes, Alice and Brad crossed the sidewalk and entered the reception hall. Although the hall was lit by a couple of small bulbs, the desk stood unattended.

'No register either,' Brad remarked. 'Well, if we can't sleep why should anybody else. Will you jab the bell, boss lady, or do I?'

'Power hasn't corrupted me yet,' she replied, and jabbed her thumb on the desk's bell-push.

The door behind the desk opened and a bleary eyed man came out. While he wore a well-tailored, sober suit, his shirt's neck was open and his tie drawn down.

'Yes?' he asked coldly, dropping suspicious eyes to Alice's ring-less left hand.

'No,' she replied, and flipped open her ID wallet. 'We're deputies. Is Mr Jackson still here?'

'Jackson?' repeated the young man, setting up a plaque

announcing that Mr S. Silverman held post as night manager. 'Is he a resident?'

'He booked an air-line flight from here,' Brad answered. 'Maybe he only came in to use the phone.'

'Check the register, please, Mr Silverman,' Alice went on.

Taking the register from under the desk, Silverman flipped it open and ran a finger down the column of names on page.

'Mr Otis B. Jackson?'

'The same,' agreed Alice.

'He checked out this evening.'

'What time?' Brad asked.

'I came on at eight and he had gone by then.'

'When did he check in?' Alice inquired.

'Friday afternoon. What's he done?'

'Should he have done anything?' smiled Alice.

Then Silverman got it. While the sheriff's office personnel had county-wide jurisdiction, they left most investigations in Gusher City to the Detective Bureau. Silverman owned a radio and listened to it, so he could guess at what brought the two deputies to disturb his sleep.

'Was he a regular guest, sir?' Brad asked.

'This's his first time here,' Silverman replied.

'What did he look like?' Alice asked.

'Tall, jovial, burly. He said he was a salesman, but didn't mention what he sold. A bell-hop told me about him, said Mr Jackson had a gun-case along and was going on vacation after he finished his business in town.'

'Can I use your phone?' asked Alice.

'Feel free. Say, is he involved in——'

Before the man could frame the end of his question, Alice had taken up the telephone and started to dial the office's number.

'We've hit pay dirt, I think,' she said when the sheriff answered. 'He fits the description and had a gun along. What'll we do?'

'Is he there still?'

'Left some time this afternoon.'

'Stay on, I'll have a lab crew sent over. Has the room been touched since he left?'

On raising Jack's query, Alice discovered that the hotel's cleaning staff came on at seven in the morning. When Alice relayed the information, Jack repeated his orders for the deputies to stay put and said he would send a lab crew to join them.

'We'll try not to disturb your other guests, Mr Silverman,' Alice promised in her most winning manner. 'Would it be possible to check if Mr Jackson had any visitors, or sent and received any phone calls during his stay?'

'You could ask around the staff when they come on,' the man replied. 'They might remember. He had nobody to see him while I was on duty. We keep a record only of out-going calls, but again the switchboard girl might help you. She comes in at nine—when she's not late.'

'We'll come around and see her,' Alice told Brad and he nodded.

Half an hour later a trio of technicians of the Scientific Investigation Bureau arrived at the Newnes and were escorted to the room 'Jackson' had occupied. First the Latent Prints Detail's representative went over the room, using his considerable knowledge in an attempt to find fingerprints left by the occupant. A significant point came from the check.

'There's not a print to be found,' the expert told Alice and Brad. 'And I know that nobody uses a room for three days without leaving a few. That room's been gone over with a rag the way my wife's mother goes over the sitting-room.'

'The cleaning staff didn't do it,' Alice breathed. 'Let the lab crew have a look while I call in.'

'We've hit pay dirt, Alice,' Jack told the girl when she reported the discovery. 'Ian called from the Bestwick. Sloane fits the other guy, and his room had been cleaned—only he wasn't as thorough as Jackson. They raised a full set from the inside of the wash-basin cabinet's door.'

'It could be——' Alice said.

'Sure, it could be,' agreed Jack. 'I'm having the prints rushed back here and flown up to I.C.R., they'll Speedphoto them through to the F.B.I. and ask for a top priority make. You and Brad can come in, leave the lab crew to finish.'

One of the lab crew appeared at Alice's side, bringing news that they had found no scientific evidence in the room, even the waste-paper basket and ashtrays had been emptied, the latter cleaned out of ash even. No innocent man would go to such lengths before leaving a hotel.

'You know, Alice,' Brad said as they drove back to the office. 'One thing bugs me. The job was so well organised, the killers acted so careful. Yet they made a damned fool mistake like booking those flights then not showing to take them.'

'They knew we'd be covering the airport as soon as we heard about Tom's death,' Alice pointed out.

'Then why make the reservations in the first place?' asked Brad, just as the same thought hit Alice.

Although neither of the deputies realised it, Brad had just asked a question the answer of which would solve the reason behind Tom's killing.

CHAPTER NINE

'It's about time they gave us a room downstairs,' Woman Deputy Joan Hilton remarked, watching Alice don a dark blue pencil line skirt after washing and making up her face in the women's room on the fourth floor of Headquarters Building. 'They could convert the waiting-room for us.'

'And use the tax-payer's money just so a few female deputies don't need to walk to an elevator?' Alice replied, drawing up the skirt's zip. 'I can't see the County Commissioners buying that.'

'Or me. I hope I brought you the right outfit from the apartment.'

'Sure, thanks, Joan.'

The time was eight o'clock on Monday morning and Joan had just logged on day watch. Due to her place being re-decorated, Joan was rooming with Alice and had fetched along a change of clothing for her friend. Deputies normally worked in plain clothes when investigating in town, so Joan selected Alice's dark, stylish two-piece and a plain white blouse.

'Did you get any sleep last night?' Joan went on while Alice finished dressing.

'Some. All the boys were so considerate. Brad fetched me a camp bed and blankets from the locker room and I bunked down in the squadroom.'

'Anything new?' asked Joan, getting on to the case at last.

'Not yet. We found one set of prints and got them off to I.C.R. Hey though, Mick and Tommy picked up Salvador Amarez on a 1391.'

'How come?' Joan inquired, knowing there must be more to the story than the arrest of a known criminal who had often been brought in and charged under Article 1391 of the Penal Code: burglary of a private residence.

'They were prowling and remembered Uncle Tom put the arm on Amarez and sent him down for a three-stretch. Amarez made some threats at the time. So they went to his pad, this being around three in the morning. When they knocked, the light they'd seen under the door went out. So they broke in. From what they said, it must have been quite a sight. There was Amarez trying to get out of the window, wearing his street clothes. But his girl-friend, and from the way Tom described her, thinking I was sound asleep in my little bed, she made Jayne Mansfield look as slim as Leslie Caron, was standing in the middle of the room—wearing a mink wrap, and nothing else.'

'What happened?'

'It seems that Amarez hit a house in Upton Heights and the wrap was part of the take. The girl had never worn one, so he let her try it. The boys brought her in still wearing it.'

'What?' gasped Joan.

'Oh, they let her dress first,' smiled Alice. 'The rest of the boys did look disappointed. Mick contacted the owner of the house Amarez hit and he didn't even know his property had gone.'

'Did Amarez make trouble?'

'Would you with a couple of .41 Magnums pointed at your favourite navel?'

'Do you think he was tied in with the hit on Tom?' Joan asked, conceding Alice's point.

'Not if Brad's theory about imported professionals is right. Amarez was just out of the Eastham Unit[1] a week back and not holding much. He couldn't have paid for a contract, those boys don't work on time.'

'He wouldn't've pulled a job the same night if he had hired it done,' Joan remarked. 'Amarez might not be smart, but he's smart enough to know we'd be looking for him.'

'Just like Goole,' agreed Alice, finishing snapping her suspender belt's last strap to a stocking. 'Let's get to the elevators before they're crowded.'

The fourth floor of the building belonged to the Scientific Investigation Bureau and on leaving the women's room Alice saw two S.I.B. men entering an elevator.

[1] *Eastham Unit: State Prison Farm, Weldon, Texas.*

'Hey!' she called. 'Down?'

'Down,' agreed the taller man and held open the doors. 'Sorry to hear about Tom, Alice. Any leads?'

'Nothing much,' Alice admitted. 'And what's taking the pride of the Arson Detail out into the chill morning air?'

'A fire,' grinned the second man.

'No!' Joan gasped.

'Garage on Jenner Street, down in the Bad-Bit. Call's just come in.'

'Maybe the Fire Chief wants two more for a game of bridge,' Alice suggested.

'He'd've called the sheriff's office if he did,' replied the taller man.

Before either deputy could think up an adequate answer the lift reached the third floor and its doors opened. Waving a hand to the two detectives, Alice led the way to the squad-room. First Deputy Alvarez looked out of his office as the girls entered to sign the log book at the right of the main doors.

'The El Paso Police Department called,' he said. 'Greer's at the hotel, been there since Friday. The hotel staff know him.'

'Which leaves him in the clear,' Alice commented and went to her desk. A sheet of paper lay on it and she read, 'Latent Prints, no make on set found at the Bestwick. That figures. Hey, Ric, Brad and I'll grab a bite at the Badge and start running down some leads.'

Then Alice fell silent and dropped her eyes to the desk top. One of the leads to follow entailed questioning her aunt. Knowing how Tom and Mavis Cord had loved each other, Alice hated the thought of the painful interview to come. Yet she had asked to be assigned to the case and must handle every aspect of it, no matter how painful the duty proved.

Brad entered the squadroom. It appeared that he had risen earlier than his partner, and had been across town to his apartment, for he was clean shaven and wore a sports jacket, dark grey open necked shirt, black cravat and grey slacks. Instead of carrying his gun on the official belt, he now wore a Hardy-Cooper spring shoulder holster and it would have taken keen eyes to detect the bulge of the big automatic under his left arm.

'Let's go eat,' he suggested after glancing at the Latent Prints' negative report and the pile of cards sent up by the Stats. Office. 'We'll start on them after we get back.'

'Sure. We've a busy day ahead, Brad.'

The Badge Diner lay a block away from Headquarters Building, but it drew most of the sheriff's office and police trade. Owned by an ex-cop, retired through a wound gained during the big clean-up of the county, the Badge served good food and offered a handy place to eat while still being close to the House in case of emergency. Several off-watch policemen and women sat around the room as Alice and Brad entered. For a moment the laughter and chatter died, then rose again although with a slightly strained note added. Hank Seaborn, the owner, came across to the deputies' table, only a slight limp showing that he had an artificial leg.

'Sorry to hear about Tom,' he said. 'What'll it be?'

'Ham, eggs, coffee for two,' Brad said. 'That do, boss lady?'

'Do fine,' Alice confirmed.

They had finished their breakfasts and sat over a second cup of coffee when Seaborn called, 'Telephone, Alice.'

Rising, the deputies crossed the room and Alice took the telephone receiver Seaborn offered her. She listened to the message and said, 'We'll be right over, Pete.' Handing the receiver back to Seaborn, she turned to Brad and went on, 'That was Pete Kajic of Arson. He wants us to go down to Jenner Street. As far as he can tell, there's the remains of a repeating shotgun in a burned-out car that could be a Plymouth Fury. And they've found the body of a man by the car.'

'We'll get right over,' Brad replied. 'Who's paying the check—— Oh, all right, so pull rank. I'll pay it, but I'll write my congressman.'

Suddenly Brad realised he would have made exactly the same remark had he been sharing a meal with Tom Cord. His eyes went to Alice and she smiled, guessing his thoughts.

On returning to Headquarters, the deputies took car SO 12 and, with Alice at the wheel, drove out of the official vehicles parking lot. Brad called the dispatcher and notified her of where they intended to go, and Alice took the shortest route to Jenner Street.

Lying on the fringe of the Bad-Bit, Gusher City's sprawling slum area, Jenner Street was a business section and the garage proved to be a single-storey building separated from its neighbours by an alley on either side. People crowded the sidewalk, controlled by patrolmen who had been rushed over from the Evans Park Station House. A Fire Department engine and trailer stood before the building, firemen coiling their hoses. Beyond the engine were a couple of R.P. cars, a D car and the Arson Detail's truck. A couple of detectives stood questioning a big, buxom woman on the fringe of one of the sections of the crowd.

Bringing the Oldsmobile to a halt before the truck, Alice climbed out and joined Brad on the sidewalk. Each had their badge pinned on in plain sight and went down the alley to where they could see Pete Kajic, the taller of the two men Alice had met in the elevator.

'I thought you'd want to come down,' Kajic remarked. He now wore smoke and grease-stained overalls and his face had a couple of smudges on it. 'As near as we can tell, the car's a Fury. You'd best stay out here, Alice.'

'Is it as bad as that?' she asked.

'They always are,' grunted Kajic.

'Anyways,' Brad went on. 'What's the use in bossing the team if you can't let your underling do all the dirty work?'

Alice smiled and did not make a stand on female equality. Having worked on Traffic, mangled bodies no longer struck her as a novelty and she knew Brad would see everything she could. So she stood back and let her partner enter the side door of the building.

'It's a torch job,' Kajic remarked as he and Brad entered the burned-out workshop. 'Not a top-flight professional one though. I'd say they used a simple time fuse, say a candle burning down towards a bundle of petrol-soaked rags or paper. Everything in here, including the body, had been soaked in petrol. There was some paint-spraying equipment and the paint aided the blaze.'

'Why don't you reckon it's a top professional job?' asked Brad, not looking at the blackened, twisted shape on the floor after his first glance.

'Instinct more than anything,' Kajic admitted. 'They only

made one starting point. Good torch men would have made three or four flash points. The fire took hold pretty well before being seen, but not as good as the guy who set it hoped. The drapes caught fire, broke the windows and gave the alarm. Professionals would have made certain that that didn't happen so quickly.'

'Any damage at the rear?' Brad inquired, holding off from the unpleasant business of studying the body.

'Not much. The bed's been slept on, not in. I've sent for an S.I.B. crew. Look inside the car.'

Brad obeyed, and saw the remains of a gun, its wood-work badly burned, the breech and tube magazine shattered by the exploding of heated shells.

'Can I?' he asked, reaching inside and taking out the remains. 'Rifle sights, but it's a shotgun, the bore's too large for a rifle. Twenty inch barrel, built for ball and buckshot.'

'Sure. Want to take a look at the stiff?'

'Nope—but I have to.'

Only by an effort did Brad hold down an exclamation of revulsion as he looked at the body. Contracted by the heat, the body's muscles caused the arms and legs to bend into an attitude as though it had been fighting for its life when struck down by the flames. It looked like a grotesque caricature of a human being.

'How tall do you reckon he was in life?' Brad asked, turning away.

'Five seven, eight at most, stocky build,' Kajic answered. 'May be the owner, he's not around this morning. I can't say whether the flames got him or how he died. The M.E.'ll have to give you that.'

'Brad!' Alice called from the passage door. 'Have you finished?'

'Sure,' Brad replied and walked to her side. He did not look unhappy at leaving the room.

'The local fuzz found a woman who might be able to help us.'

'And she'll talk?' asked Brad. 'I thought folks in the Bad-Bit were born deaf, dumb and with built-in seeing-eye dogs.'

'Don't be bitter,' Alice warned. 'There're nice folks everywhere.'

The big, buxom woman, clearly of Mexican descent, stood waiting on the street, a detective at her side.

'This's Mrs Mendoza,' the detective introduced. 'Tell these folks what you-all told me, Rosa.'

'Say, are you a cop?' asked the woman, looking Alice over and speaking with no trace of an accent.

'Deputy sheriff,' Alice confirmed. 'Did you know the owner of the garage, Mrs Mendoza?'

'Frankie Thurlow? Sure, I know him. I've got a fruit and vegetable store across the street. He comes to buy my stuff, I give him all my repair work like good neighbours. I tell you, Frankie can re-paint a truck faster than any guy in town.'

'He did respray work then?' asked Alice.

'Sure, plenty of it.'

'About how tall is Mr Thurlow?' Brad inquired.

'About five nine—— Say, is he in there?'

'There's a body inside, but it's unidentifiable. Can you tell us anything about his background?'

'Not much. He bought the place two years back, reckoned he'd been in the Quartermaster Corps in Korea.'

'Was he doing all right?' Alice put in. 'Financially, I mean.'

'Sure, I reckon he was. He always had plenty of work. Say, do you reckon that feller I saw knows anything about the fire?'

'Which man?' asked Alice, dropping the subject of the spray-job. The G.C.P.D. could handle that aspect of the business.

'He came down the alley there at about half past seven,' Mrs Mendoza replied. 'I was just opening the store, you know, I catch folks going to work, do a good bit of trade that way. Anyway, I saw him come out of the alley, thought he might have come through from North Jenner.'

'What did he look like?' Brad asked.

'Biggish, heavy build, tanned, not——'

'How did he dress?' Alice interrupted.

'Dark suit, fedora, carrying a suitcase.'

Alice and Brad exchanged glances. Then the girl turned to Mrs Mendoza. 'Can you come down to Headquarters, please?' she asked.

'Is it important?'

'It may be. We'd like you to look at some photographs, and

try to build up a picture of the man. One of our artists will work with you.'

'Did he kill Frankie and fire the garage?' growled Mrs Mendoza.

'We don't know,' Alice admitted. 'But it's possible.'

'Then I'll do it!' the woman stated. 'Hell, Frankie was a good neighbour. I'll tell my man to tend to the store.'

'Thanks, Mrs Mendoza,' Alice replied. 'Brad, arrange for a car to take Mrs Mendoza to the office.'

'Yo!' Brad answered.

Watching the big deputy walk away, Mrs Mendoza grinned and nudged Alice with her elbow. 'Now I see why you became a cop,' she chuckled. 'That's quite a hunk of man.'

Alice smiled. 'I never thought of it like that—but you've a point.'

CHAPTER TEN

AFTER seeing Mrs Mendoza on her way, Alice and Brad asked Kajic to keep in touch with them and took to their car. During the drive to Tom Cord's home, more to take their minds off what lay ahead, they kicked around what they had learned at Jenner Street. Both agreed that the fire tied in with their case and their guessing came very close to the true reason for the arson—murder, and attempted destruction of the shotgun and car.

At the Cord house Alice and Brad found a grief-stricken woman; forcing themselves to follow the routine course of questioning. Despite her grief, Mavis Cord realised the deputies had a job to do, and also that her help might give a clue to the reason for her husband's death.

Did Mavis know of any enemies, other than the usual kind gathered by a peace officer, who might have wanted Tom's death? Had he quarrelled with the neighbours? Who knew of his whereabouts on Sunday?

Alice and Brad knew, or could guess, most of the answers.

Off watch Tom had been an amiable, home-loving man; possibly because he saw so little of it when working on a case, or came across so many contrasts to his own matrimonial state in the line of duty. Apart from very rare domestic spats, he got on well enough with his neighbours and Mavis could not think of a single enemy, other than criminals, who could have hired the killing of her husband.

'Nothing,' Alice said as they left the house.

'No,' Brad agreed. 'I'm pleased that Mrs Tragg's there with Mavis.'

The sheriff's capable wife had stayed on to take care of the grieving woman. Knowing Beryl Tragg, Alice and Brad felt Mavis could not be in better hands. With the welfare of Tom's and Brad could get on with their

From the Cord house Alice and Brad ranged across the city, calling on men Tom had arrested, asking questions, checking alibis. They learned nothing and after lunch split up to make a round of their informers.

Brad used his M.G., visiting the men who sold Tom Cord information. He spoke with English Herb and Joey Ortega in the Bad-Bit, visited a poolroom in Greevers where Stan Bauman could be found, called on Stan Weiss' shoe-shine stand and lastly went to Izzy Bergen's junk yard.

From none of the men did he learn anything useful, but all had started to dig information. Most of them believed Tom's death to be a grudge-killing and acted accordingly. Only two things came of Brad's inquiries. First, although he knew it already, that Tom had been genuinely liked and respected by his informers; second, and very important, the old deputy had planned against his retirement by arranging for the informers to adopt Brad as his successor for a market for news. All agreed to continue working for Brad; an important detail since every peace officer needed such unofficial sources of information to augment the scientific aids to his work.

'Tom allus said I could rely on you like I did on him,' Bergen said, echoing the other informers' sentiments. 'I'll call you if I get a whisper.'

'Thanks Izzy, I'll see you around.'

With that side of the investigation handled, Brad drove back to Headquarters Building and found, from the pile of reports on his desk, that other sections of the search had also gone on at full pace.

I.C.R. in Austin could not trace the fingerprints from the Bestwick in their collection, but had Speedphoto'ed them and dispatched the result over the wire service to the Federal Bureau of Investigation's Identification Division for further checking at national level. So far the F.B.I. had not kicked back a report. With Alice and Brad so busy, a G.C.P.D. detective visited the Newnes to question the staff. He reported that 'Jackson' had received no visitors, only one telephone call at around half past four on Sunday afternoon and that after receiving it had left the hotel for a few minutes. A preliminary report from the medical examiner's office declared that the Jenner Street victim had been male and had died as a result of three bullet wounds; one bullet proved to be suitable for comparison tests should the deputies locate a .45-calibre revolver. F.I.L. had received the bullet and passed word that it came from a Smith & Wesson; they also said that Goole's shotgun had not been fired for several days. In addition to Mrs Mendoza, staff-members from the two hotels worked with police artists to build up a composite sketch of 'Sloane' and 'Jackson'. S.I.B.'s investigations at the garage produced a set of licence plates which were partially eaten away by acid, but which might yield to treatment and show the obliterated number. The lab crew decided to check on the electric razor found in Thurlow's room, a fortunate decision as it proved to have three different types of hair in its cutter-blades. Following up the lead, the lab crew brought in the pillow from Thurlow's bed and tested it for samples of hair-oil, bringing in the pillows from 'Jackson' and 'Sloane's' hotel rooms for comparison. As a result of appeals on the radio and television newscasts, passengers from the nine-fifty train started reporting to their local station houses, but so far nobody who resembled Tom in height and appearance had turned up. The train's crew had gone straight on to Arizona, but would be returning that evening, so could be questioned.

'Short and sweet,' Brad said, putting down the last report.

'Aren't they all?' Alice replied. Having returned before Brad, she sat at the desk typing out a report of the case so far.

'We're further forward though,' Brad remarked.

'A little,' agreed Alice, and reached out a hand as the telephone buzzed. 'Sheriff's office, Deputy Fayde.'

'This's Craddock, R. and I. We've just found a hot one.'

'Shoot,' she said, taking up her pencil.

'Zachary Rosenthal. Tom put him away for fifteen years on a 1398.[1] That was eight years back, which's why we've only just found it. Rosenthal made a lot of threats at the time.'

'Is he out?'

'Of this world, though I wouldn't want to say up or down.

[1] *1398: Article 1398, Texas Penal Code, burglary in which explosives were used.*

He died in the Walls[1] three weeks ago.'

'That's a reasonable alibi,' Brad remarked, listening with his head close to his partner's shoulder.

'Yeah,' Craddock replied. 'Only he had a son. Boy figured he was some red-hot high-power. Took a couple of 1148 falls and one for armed robbery.'

'Sounds like a clean-cut American boy,' Alice said dryly. 'Is he out?'

'Out and in gainful employment. According to his parole report, he's working as a chauffer for an Upton Heights family.'

'Do they know about him?' Alice asked, for most people fought shy of hiring a young man who had been in jail on an Article 1148 charge—aggravated assault.

'Sure. Reckon the man of the house figures he can handle a young punk like Rosenthal. It's Stan Blumfeld.'

From Craddock's tone the name should mean something to the listening deputies. It struck no bell and Alice said so.

'He's a retired gambling biggie out of Las Vegas. Came to live here around eighteen month back,' Craddock told them. 'Jack went to see him when he arrived, told him we weren't having any organised gambling in Rockabye County. V. and G. have had him under surveillance but he acts clean. Is an exec. in Cowland Footwear.'

'Then we'll run over and see Blumfeld,' Alice remarked. If the young man's employer had not been aware of his past, she would have suggested a meeting away from his place of employment. 'Thanks for the tip.'

'That's what we're here for,' replied Craddock and hung up.

'What do you think, Brad?' Alice asked, putting the receiver on its hooks.

'Don't like it. Sure Blumfeld had the motive, but would he have the means; enough money to hire the professionals?'

'He could have been one of the "professionals",' Alice pointed out. 'He'd have the local knowledge and might still be in contact with his old crowd.'

'Sure,' Brad grunted. 'I may have become a bit too set on that professional killer bit. We'd best check him out.'

'We'll have to go by the Chadwick Building on the way,'

[1] *The Walls: Main State Prison, Huntsville, Texas.*

Alice remarked as they left the office. 'I'll call in and pick up my car. I came by taxi last night and if I manage to get home tonight, it'll be hell finding a cab at that hour.'

'I could run you home if you like,' suggested Brad.

'You live on the other side of the Heights, it would take you well out of your way.'

There the matter rested. Alice and Brad had never been close friends off watch. While they saw each other around town occasionally, each possessed a circle of friends who had little in common with the other's.

On arriving at the Chadwick Building, a white stone structure in the middle-rent district, Alice left the Oldsmobile and collected her cobalt blue '64 Ford Mustang hardtop from the roofed-over parking lot. She drove from the lot, waved to Brad and led the way across town, making for Upton Street, boundary of the snob Upton Heights Division.

The quality, appearance and value of the property they passed had been gradually increasing as they drove north from Alice's place. Once across Upton Street, which encircled the small hill range known as Upton Heights, they would be in the richest area of the town. Before leaving the office Alice had checked on Blumfeld's address, finding it to be on Beunavista Avenue. Streets wound around the Heights like the contour lines of a map and the higher one went, the more select and expensive grew the section. Beunavista Avenue lay second from the top.

Although all of Upton Heights, and indeed most of Gusher City, had risen since the big oil-boom in 1940, the houses on Beunavista Avenue had been built to give an impression of antiquity. The Blumfeld residence proved to be a three-storey pseudo Spanish-colonial design. High walls surrounded it and almost a hundred yards of well-tended lawns and flower beds separated the building from the street. From the ornate wrought-iron gates two paths curved off across the lawns to join again in an oblong of concrete almost as large as the Chadwick Building's parking lot and facing the main doors of the building.

Alice swung her Ford through the gate and, with Brad following in SO 12, cruised along the right-hand path. A powder blue Cadillac Sedan de Ville and a matching Lotus

Elite Gran Turismo coupé stood side by side on the square. There would probably be at least two more cars in the garages at the rear of the building. Possibly the pair out front belonged to the lady of the house; the little imported coupé for casual use and driven by herself, but the Cadillac called for the services of a chauffeur. A cleaning cloth hung over the door of the Lotus, but there was no sign of the chauffeur.

'I feel we should be using the tradesmen's entrance,' Alice said, looking around her.

She was conscious of the fact that her two-piece and blouse did not look at their neatest after several hours of riding in the Oldsmobile and visiting a variety of unsavoury places around town. Woman-like, Alice did not wish to appear before the female occupants of such a place while not looking at her best.

Having been reared in similar surroundings, Brad showed no concern. He grinned at his partner and answered, 'Let's make a stand for equality and rights of the individual, and use the front door.'

'We can't. Rights of the individual only apply to members of minority groups. Don't you watch television?'

'Not since the westerns all stopped shooting and went psycho. Let's go.'

A tall, frozen-faced man with the appearance of a butler in a 'B' movie opened the main doors in answer to Brad's tug on the bell-pull. After giving Alice a quick look, the man asked whom they wished to see.

'Your chauffeur,' Alice replied, face deadpan.

'Whom may I say is——' began the butler.

'Knock it off, Weems,' Alice interrupted and reached for her ID wallet. 'Or don't you remember me?'

'Miss Fayde, isn't it?' answered the man in his aloof tones.

'They said you never forgot a face,' she commented with a smile.

'There are some one would wish to forget, miss. No offence meant, of course, I found no complaint in your attention. By the by, miss, the master is fully cognizant with my previous lapse from grace. In other words, to use the vernacular, I'm going straight now.'

'Don't let it worry you, it happens to the best of us in the end.'

'Regrettable, but true,' sighed the butler. 'And the younger generation leave so much to be desired.'

'Talking of the younger generation——' Alice said.

'You wish to speak with Rosenthal?'

'If I can.'

'He's with the mistress. I'll inform him.'

With that the butler waved the deputies inside and padded off along the hall to a door.

'Man'd say you know that jasper, Alice,' Brad remarked.

'Who, Weems? I met him while I was a patrolwoman out of Upton Heights's House. An informer blew the whistle on a big-time fence and I went along on the raid. We hit the fence just as Weems was selling him a mink wrap lifted from a guest at his employer's place. The fence sang like a bird, trying to lighten his load, and made poor old Weems. There'd been a lot of thefts in the Heights at that time and Weems was the guilty party. He went down for three; and six months later I met his employer's wife. She said she wished she'd never signed the complaint as she hadn't seen a butler to touch him.'

'There's a moral in that somewhere,' grinned Brad. 'Say, though. Weems and Rosenthal are both ex-cons, and Blumfeld hired them.'

'Maybe he has a social conscience,' Alice suggested. 'Or finds ex-cons other folks wouldn't hire come cheaper than honest help.'

Before they could discuss the matter further, Weems reappeared. 'Mrs Blumfeld says come this way, please.'

The room into which Weems showed the deputies had the same air of wealth and elegance which filled the rest of the house. At the far wall stood a divan almost as large as a double bed and at its side was a small table bearing a crystal glass whiskey decanter, two partly-filled glasses and an onyx ashtray with several cigarette butts in it; not all the butts bore traces of lipstick.

A young man and a slightly older woman stood by the divan and studied the deputies as Alice and Brad crossed the room.

The man was almost as tall as Brad, tanned and handsome, with broad shoulders set off by a chauffeur's tunic. From all appearances, he was not in the room on official business. The cadet-grey jacket hung open, showing a white T-shirt. A cigarette trailed from lips which bore a street-punk's tough sneer. Just a trace of the same shade of lipstick that marked some of the cigarette butts in the ashtray stained the corner of his mouth.

Standing at Rosenthal's side, the woman's eyes narrowed slightly as she gave Alice a long, hard stare.

Although not quite as tall as Alice, the woman's gold-coloured, sling back court shoes gave the impression that they were the same height. She had blonde hair elegantly coiffured in a bouffant style and framing a beautiful face with slightly pouting lips. A white sheath dress clung like it had been moulded to her magnificent figure, the neck-line cut low enough over her rich full bosom to start Brad wondering if she wore any underclothes. Full breasted, with a slender waist, curving hips and legs which would turn heads against any competition, the woman looked more like a Hollywood sex-queen than an Upton Heights housewife interviewing her chauffeur. She wore pendant diamond earrings, a wide silver bracelet on her right wrist. A broad wedding band and a second ring with a large diamond cluster rising like a pyramid graced the third finger of her left hand.

Recognition came to both women at the same moment.

'Hello, Alice,' said the blonde in a voice which dripped sex like a melting candle sheds wax.

'Hello, Marla,' Alice replied.

Something in the two voices drew Brad's attention to the woman. He studied the way they stood and felt that the attitude should be familiar to him. The tense, watchful, somehow predatory way the women eyed each other struck a chord in Brad's memory, but he could not quite place it.

Then he remembered.

It had been up on the family's ranch in the Panhandle when he was out hunting. While stalking through the woods in search of a big whitetail buck, he came upon a rare sight. A log bridged a small, swift stream and two bobcats stood upon it facing each other. Neither cat showed any signs of backing down and letting the other pass.

The way Alice faced Marla Blumfeld reminded Brad of how the bobcats stood bristling and eyeing each other before the fight started and fur began to fly.

CHAPTER ELEVEN

'WE'D like to see Mr Rosenthal,' Brad said, for Alice made no attempt to open the interview.

'Go right ahead,' Marla answered.

'Could we speak with him in private, please?'

'There's nothing you can say to me that Mar—Mrs Blumfeld can't hear,' Rosenthal put in. 'Make with the talk, cop.'

'We'd rather see you alone,' Brad replied.

'And I'd rather you didn't,' Marla put in. 'I know Ben has been in trouble with the law—which only means he didn't have the right connections.'

'Or that he was guilty,' Alice said.

Once again the sparks flew between the women. Brad felt surprised at Alice's reaction, for normally no amount of needling would bring such a comment from her. Yet she stood bristling like an alley-cat—and so did Marla.

'You may as well question him here, I have no intention of leaving him,' Marla announced.

Alice writhed under the blonde's faintly mocking scrutiny of her clothes. Of all the people in the world, the woman who called herself Marla Blumfeld would have been the last Alice chose to meet when not dressed at her best.

'Where were you yesterday evening at nine-fifty, Mr Rosenthal?' Brad asked when Alice did not start the questioning.

For an instant something flickered and wiped the mocking sneer from Rosenthal's face. Brad saw it. Alice, watching Marla, also caught a fleeting glimpse of a change. The air of mocking condescension went, was replaced by another expression and returned slightly diminished.

Had fear caused the change? Apprehension at what answer might be given? The lipstick stain on Rosenthal's mouth and the two obviously used glasses might supply a reason for the change in Marla, hinting as they did at a far closer relationship than that of employer's wife and chauffeur.

'Who wants to know?' Rosenthal snarled in his hard-case's voice.

'Here or at the sheriff's office?' Brad countered.

'Huh?' grunted the chauffeur.

'Do you answer here, or at the office? We want to know where you were last night at nine-fifty.'

'Tell them the truth, Ben,' Marla put in quietly.

Rosenthal's eyes swung towards her. For a moment he showed surprise, his mouth hanging open and the cigarette dropping to the expensive wall-to-wall carpet. Clearly he had not expected Marla to make such a suggestion.

'What would be the truth, Rosenthal?' Brad asked.

'I'm afraid Ben has been a naughty boy,' Marla purred before the chauffeur could reply. 'It was his weekend off and he took my Lotus—and before you start making a Federal case out of it, both my husband and I allow Ben the use of our cars—— Well, Ben took my Lotus——'

'Suppose we let him tell it, Mrs Blumfeld,' Alice cut in.

'Whatever you say, dear. And you can call me "Marla". I'm still the same girl even though I have—well, you know what I mean.'

A slight tinge of red crept into Alice's cheeks and she looked at Rosenthal.

'Sure, I took the Lotus,' the chauffeur said.

'Where'd you go?'

'Up to Brazoria.'

'That's a fair piece from here. When'd you go?'

'Left Friday at noon,' Rosenthal replied, throwing glances at Marla.

'Why'd you go?'

'See a gal I know there.'

'Name?'

'Huh?'

'Knock it off, Rosenthal,' Brad snapped. 'You know the routine——'

'I think I'd better call my husband's lawyer,' Marla put in. 'You seem to be exceeding your authority.'

'He can answer here or at the office, ma'am,' Brad answered.

'Her name was Dodo, well that's what we called her. She worked at the Rancho Grande, only she'd left.'

'Where'd you stay in Brazoria?' asked Alice.

'Buckley's Motel.'

'And when did you get back here?' Brad continued.

'This morning, man, early. Your road blocks stopped me on the State Auto Road. You can——'

'I heard Ben come back and I believe Weems may have,' Marla put in. 'Shall I call him?'

'We'll take your word,' Alice told the blonde.

'What's the beef, fuzz?' Rosenthal asked.

'Should there be a beef?' Brad inquired.

'Don't feed me that! Nine-fifty last night. That's when the badge was washed at the depot. I heard it over the newscast and read the papers.'

'Sure!' grunted Brad.

'And you're trying to make me for the kill?'

'We're making a routine——' Alice began.

'The hell you are! That badge was the one who put the arm on my old man and sent him down.'

'It was,' Brad agreed.

'And you think I'd wash a badge just for that?' Rosenthal scoffed. 'Man, you've flipped. My old man was a drunken bum who got tagged and didn't have the bread to grease a grafting fuzz.'

Sudden anger glinted in Brad's eyes. Tom Cord had been his friend and an honest peace officer who never took a dime from any man. Yet that cheap gutter-bum was accusing the old deputy of taking in a crook who could not buy his way clear.

'Knock that talk off right now!' Brad growled.

'Yeah?' sneered Rosenthal.

Then he made a mistake.

Figuring that Marla would throw her influence his way, and supply expert legal assistance to his protection, Rosenthal clenched his fist and threw a punch. It was a beautiful blow, driving out with his weight behind it. He dropped his shoulder slightly and drove his knuckles into the side of Brad's jaw, knocking the big deputy back across the room.

Gliding forward, Rosenthal walked into a backhand slap

that slammed his head to one side. He had never expected any man to take a punch from him and come back for more. Staggering a couple of paces to the rear, he caught his balance and lashed up his foot as Brad came towards him. More than one street or bar-room brawl went Rosenthal's way when he delivered such a kick. Only this time he aimed it at a trained cop, the descendant of a fighting breed, and a man who knew how to handle his end in any kind of company.

Brad's left hand stabbed down, fingers clamping on Rosenthal's kicking leg at the foot. Then the big blond swung the leg up and around, twisting on the foot. It left Rosenthal with no choice. The chauffer's other foot shot from the floor and he flipped over to land with a crash on his back.

Bending, Brad clamped hold of Rosenthal's jacket and hauled the chauffeur erect as easy as a nurse lifting a baby. Releasing the dazed man, Brad smashed a left into his belly. Rosenthal gave a croaking moan and folded over; right on to Brad's other hand as it ripped up. Jerked erect, Rosenthal pitched back, struck the wall by the door and slid down in a limp heap.

Then Brad became aware of a scuffling sound behind him.

'Let go of me!'

The words, spoken with more concentrated fury and hatred than Brad could ever remember hearing in a human voice, brought the big deputy around to look at the speaker.

Alice stood holding Marla's right arm twisted in a hammerlock with one hand, the other gripping the blonde's left ankle and holding it bent backwards and from the floor. At their feet lay the whiskey decanter.

Releasing Marla's leg, Alice thrust the blonde away from her. Marla turned, spitting out a mouthful of curses more usual from a Bad-Bit hooker than an Upton Heights socialite. She stood facing Alice, breathing hard, fingers crooked and silver-painted nails like a cat's claws when it strikes at a mouse.

For a moment Brad thought Marla would throw herself bodily at Alice with raking nails and snapping teeth. So did Alice. She stood balancing herself lightly, hands balled into hard little fists. Neither girl spoke, but hate showed on their faces; more hatred than could have sprung merely from Brad's handling of Rosenthal.

Brad knew Marla would come off much the worse if she attacked Alice, for the red head had experience in defending herself against other women. However, he also knew that nothing but trouble would come Alice's way should she be forced to rough-handle Marla. This was not the Bad-Bit, but the upper-crust Upton Heights Division. For all her language and actions, Marla was a woman of social position and not some drunken, arrest-resisting female crook.

Yet the way the two women stood glaring at each other rendered Brad speechless. There was something awesome about two really angry women, especially beautiful women like Alice and Marla, that made a man uncertain of what to do for the best.

Seconds ticked by. At any moment Marla would throw herself at Alice——

'You rang, madam?'

Never had a voice sounded so welcome to Brad's ears. The words, the very manner in which they were spoken, broke the tension. Weems stood at the door, his face and voice showing no surprise at the scene before him. For all that showed, it might have been the normal thing in the house to walk into a room and find the chauffeur lying unconscious on the floor and Weems' mistress looking as if she meant to attack another woman with tooth and claw.

Marla let out a long breath and slowly her fingers straightened out. Letting her hands unclench, Alice flashed a glance at Brad. For a full ten seconds neither woman spoke. Then Marla's arm stabbed out, pointing at Brad.

'This man attacked Rosenthal without provocation.'

'Really, madam?' Weems answered, as calmly as if Marla commented upon the condition of the weather. 'I didn't see it.'

Fury and amazement warred on Marla's face. 'You didn't——'

'Don't try that, Marla!' Alice snapped.

'Mrs Blumfeld to you—*cop*!' Marla spat back.

'All right, *Mrs* Blumfeld. Your—chauffeur,' Alice's pause between the two words was full of implication and offence, 'attacked Deputy Counter, and I prevented you striking my partner with a whiskey decanter.'

Weems coughed to draw attention to himself. 'I'm afraid I didn't see that either, miss.'

There Marla and Alice had it. Neither could use the butler as an independent witness to verify her story.

'Did you see Rosenthal last night, Weems?' Brad put in, throwing a warning look at Alice and wanting to get her out of the house before something happened which might bring her before the County Commissioners' Disciplinary Board.

'No, sir,' the butler replied. 'He came back in the early hours of the morning, around three or four I would say, having been away since Friday noon.'

'If that satisfies you!' Marla hissed. 'I want you out of my house.'

'That's all, ma'am,' Brad answered.

'Then get out so I can call a doctor to see to Benny.'

'You want to have him wash off the lipstick,' Alice put in. 'The doctor might not understand.'

For a moment Brad thought Marla would attack Alice. The blonde's face lost all its sensual attraction and looked old, vicious, hate-filled. He decided to make an effort to avert trouble and spoke without thinking.

'Tell Rosenthal something for me, ma'am. I aim to get the men who killed Tom Cord. First thing in the morning I'm seeing every contact I have and passing word through the underworld that I'll give ten thousand dollars to the man who brings me evidence that nails the man who killed him. My name's Counter, one of the oil Counters, and I can afford to do it.'

Marla's eyes swung towards the big blond deputy, studying his expensive clothes and remembering an article she read in the *Mirror* mentioning Brad's family background. With an almost visible effort she regained control of herself and her hand lifted. It shook slightly as she pointed to the door.

'Get out!'

'Do you intend reporting this incident to the I.A.B.?' Brad asked. 'The Internal Affairs Bureau. They handle complaints against county peace officers for the Commissioners.'

'No. All I want is for you to get out of my house.'

'Let's go, Alice,' Brad ordered.

Alice's eyes told him to mind his own business, but he ignored her glare. Then, with as much of an effort as Marla showed, Alice returned to normal. Swinging on her heel, she walked from the room and Brad followed.

'Where's Mr Blumfeld, Weems?' Brad asked as the butler opened the main doors for the deputies.

'In the East on business, sir, but expected home momentarily. I hope this matter goes no further, sir. The master's previous interests make him susceptible to unfavourable publicity.'

'It's over as far as I'm concerned,' Brad said, and followed Alice from the house.

Neither spoke and Brad took the lead as they drove from the Blumfeld place. However, on the way back to the office, while passing a restaurant, Brad signalled a turn and for Alice to follow him into the parking lot. Leaving her car, Alice walked to where Brad sat in the Oldsmobile calling in a 'Code Seven' to tell the dispatcher they were off watch to eat.

'I don't feel like eating,' Alice said.

'Nor do I,' Brad answered. 'But here's as good a place as any for us to sit down while you tell me what's between you and Mrs Blumfeld.'

'It's personal.'

'And I'm your partner. If I'm going to wind up before the Disciplinary Board, I want to know why. Come on inside.'

Taking Alice's arm, Brad escorted her firmly but gently into the restaurant and to an alcove clear of the other customers. After ordering a meal, Brad looked at Alice, waiting for her to begin.

'Lord, Brad,' she said. 'I thought it all ended years ago. I'd never have believed I could hold a hate for this long.'

'I figured you knew her from someplace.'

'Here in town, when I was sixteen and at Lasher High. There were a bunch of us clubbed together, about a dozen boys and girls. We necked, never went beyond kissing. Then Marla made the scene. Her mother was a widow with a little money and Marla was spoiled rotten.'

'It sounds like you didn't like her,' Brad remarked.

'We never liked each other,' Alice corrected. 'You know how

it is, Brad, there are some people you hate on sight. I think it may have stemmed from us being so different. The real hatred didn't come until a few months later. Marla threw a party and only invited two of the gang, both girls. One of them got out when she saw the way things were going. The other—well Viv never had much sense. There were a bunch of the intellectual set from Cornwall University at the party and you know what they're like. Viv found out she was going to have a baby—she took an over-dose of sleeping pills.'

'What happened then?' asked Brad as Alice's words trailed off.

'I didn't see Marla for a few weeks after Viv's death. Then one day we were down on the Rockabye River, the gang, and one of the boys started showing some photographs of girl wrestlers. Then they got us girls wrestling, just for laughs. Marla showed up, one thing led to another and she and I started struggling. The other tussles hadn't been much, we'd roll around, push and shove until one of us sat on the other and held her down. Not with Marla and I. The gang started to encourage us, until they saw how serious it was getting. It took all the boys to pull us apart. The girls helped us clean up and I told Mum some story about how I came to have a cut lip. I suppose Marla did the same about her eye, I put a mouse on it. Marla and I never spoke to each other after that. Three months later she entered a beauty contest, lying about her age, and won it. The prize included a screen-test in Hollywood and her mother took her out there.'

'Did she make it as a movie star?'

'No. Her mother died in a car crash shortly after they reached the Coast. I lost track of Marla after that.'

'Why'd you reckon Rosenthal looked so worried when I asked him about his whereabouts last night?' asked Brad.

'So did Marla,' Alice answered. 'Judging by the way she'd been entertaining him, she must be cheating on her husband. But if Rosenthal's story about his being out of town is true, that wouldn't account for it.'

'Maybe he's blackmailing her, threatening to tell Blumfeld. Only a guy like Blumfeld would play rough. So neither of them wanted him to know about Rosenthal borrowing the Lotus for a run to Rosario. Her because of her indiscretion coming out and him for fear of what Blumfeld might have done to him.'

Alice nodded in agreement. 'That's possible. A gambling biggie would know how to handle a punk like Rosenthal. Brad, thanks for getting me out of there.'

'Forget it, that's what a partner's for. Here's the food.'

After a good meal, Alice walked back to her car with a lighter step than when she entered. For the first time since leaving the Blumfeld house she felt relaxed. It was good to have a partner in whom one could confide. Yet Alice hoped she would not meet Marla again. Next time Brad might not be there to keep her in check.

CHAPTER TWELVE

On their return to the office, Alice and Brad reported to the watch commander. McCall listened to their report, which left out the trouble at the Blumfeld place, suggested they checked on Rosenthal's story and told them the latest developments. Records and Identification had sent up a few more cards of Tom's older cases, but nothing that looked even vaguely worth following up. So far the F.B.I. had not replied on the subject of the fingerprints found at the Bestwick. After much time and effort the police artists had produced sketches of 'Sloane' and 'Jackson', and copies had been circulated around the county.

At ten o'clock the train's crew arrived at the office. Although Alice and Brad questioned the railroad workers, they learned nothing. So, at shortly after eleven, McCall told them to log off watch.

Taking her car from the municipal parking lot, after leaving Brad in the office, Alice drove home. She left her car at the Chadwick Building's parking lot and entered the deserted-looking building. Entering the automatic elevator, she rode up to the first floor. The elevator's light was not working and when it stopped at her floor, Alice found that the passage also lay in darkness.

Just as she stepped from the elevator, a hand grabbed her bag. Normally she would have been holding the bag firmly, but did not expect trouble so close to home. So the bag's strap slid from her shoulder and her grabbing fingers missed it as a medium-sized, plump female shape jerked it away and tossed it aside. Fingers gripped Alice's shoulder, turning her. Through the light which filtered in from the windows at either end of the passage, Alice caught sight of another woman ahead of her, not the person who caught her shoulder. She had a vague recollection of a form clad in slacks and an anorak which effectively prevented too much of the figure showing, the raised hood covering the hair and, from the black, shapeless blur instead of white features, a veil of something covered the face. All this Alice saw as she was swung around.

A tall girl wearing a shining mock-leather coat had caught Alice's shoulder and, as the deputy came around, launched a blow with her other hand. By that time Alice had recovered from her surprise and reacted fast. Throwing up her left hand, she deflected the big girl's punch and drove her right hard into the other's belly. The girl gasped and rocked back a couple of steps, doubling over. Before Alice had a chance to follow up her right, two hands dug into her hair, tearing at it as she was swung around and sent sprawling across the passage into the other wall.

Alice managed to twist herself around and hit the wall with her back, keeping her feet, but the plump girl who threw her already sprang forward as did the veiled shape. The third attacker's fist lashed out, catching Alice just under the right eye. Pain ripped into Alice as she felt leather and under the glove a large ring. She saw that all her attackers wore gloves and knew why. A ring would cut into flesh and gather minute, but identifiable, fragments of the victim's flesh and blood. Nobody who attacked a peace officer wanted to carry away evidence which might lead to their detection.

Ignoring the pain, Alice brought up her left hand, fingers extended and together, thumb bent over the palm, in the *tegatana*, the handsword of karate. She chopped savagely, driving the edge of her hand into the plump girl's throat and causing her to halt. Again the second woman hit her, striking at her face. Alice gasped, twisted and hit back, shooting out her fist to collide with the veiled face. Even as the third attacker staggered back holding her face, Alice tried to see where her bag fell. Inside it lay salvation in the shape of the Colt Cobra, but only if Alice could reach it.

The biggest girl came in again. Thuds, gasps, squeals and curses rang out as the three women attacked the desperately fighting Alice. She gave all her efforts to preventing them getting close and to keeping her feet. Once she went down, she would be completely at their mercy.

Among its other amenities, the Chadwick Building boasted a pretty effective sound-proofing system which prevented any noise filtering into or out of its rooms. With a couple of neighbours who often gave late and rowdy parties, Alice always regarded the sound-killing as commendable—until that moment. With the three women raining kicks, slaps and punches at her, she wished that she lived in some thin-walled building where a cough could be heard three apartments away.

Just as she landed a right which knocked the veiled woman reeling, a thought struck Alice. In her room was the answer to her problem. Joan Hilton, that tough, capable woman deputy, shared Alice's apartment and slept on the divan in the sitting-room. With Joan's able backing, Alice reckoned she could handle the three attackers. The trouble being how could she alert Joan?

Ducking under a roundhouse swing aimed by the biggest of the trio, Alice ripped a punch into a big breast. She hit hard and the big woman croaked in pain, stumbling back. That left the way clear and Alice sprang along the wall, her fingers reaching out to jab home the bell-push by her door. The plump girl came in, grabbing Alice's hair again, tearing at it, sending fire shooting through the deputy's head. Pain forced Alice to move her finger, then thought returned and she delivered a stamping kick which ripped the edge of her shoe's inner-sole down the plump shin. Screeching, the girl released her hold of Alice's hair. Once again Alice jabbed the bell.

Mouthing curses, the plump girl sprang forward, fingers reaching out. Alice left the bell, jumping forward and letting the plump girl shoot by her. The biggest girl dived forward, locking her arms around Alice's waist and the weight brought both of them crashing to the ground.

At that moment the apartment door opened, light flooding out, as Joan—a robe draped over her pyjama-clad shoulders—appeared. The blonde took one look and started forward. Lunging in, the plump girl's fist caught Joan on the cheek and sent her crashing into the door jamb. Freshly woken from sleep though she might be, Joan still knew how to handle that kind of treatment. Pivoting, she sank her left hand almost wrist-deep in her attacker's plump belly. Joan knew how to hit, in fact she could handle herself as well as many a boxer. Caught by a hard punch, the plump girl gave a croaking gasp, clutched at her middle and folded over. Before she could go to her knees, retching in nausea, Joan hit her again, ripping another blow that landed on the girl's jaw and pitched her across the passage. Hitting the other wall head-first, the plump girl went limp and dropped to the floor.

Also on the floor, thrashing over and over with the biggest girl, Alice saw the third figure turn and dart away. In fact the last of the trio started to run the moment the door opened. Rolling the big girl on to her back, Alice knelt astride her and smashed a punch to her jaw.

'Get the——!' Alice began to yell, but the big girl's back arched in an attempt to roll the burden from her.

Joan sprang to help Alice, for she had not seen the fleeing woman. With a heave, the big girl threw Alice off balance just as the deputy tried to rise. Coming to her knees, the big girl saw her own danger a moment too late. Joan halted and drew off a right hand blow that would have made any boxing trainer's heart bound in admiration. Round and up it came, catching the big girl under her chin, lifting her erect and throwing her backwards to land across the body of her friend.

Coming to her feet, Alice staggered to where her bag lay. 'H-hold them, Joan!' she gasped. 'I'm going after—other!'

Before Joan could answer, Alice bent, scooped up her bag and ran along the passage towards the stairs. Joan watched her friend go, then walked to where the two girls lay. Bending, she took a firm hold of each girl's hair and hauled them after her into the apartment, closing the door behind her.

Pain knifed through Alice as she started down the stairs. Her right eye throbbed and seemed puffed-up from the blow; blood clogged her nostrils and her top lip seemed twice its normal size; her body ached and stung where fists landed and each leg appeared to be vying with the other in pain from kicks. Gritting her teeth, she forced herself to run down the stairs, but already the foot-falls of the fleeing woman had faded off.

On reaching the ground floor, Alice halted for a moment then ran towards the front doors. She stepped out on to the street and looked around, but could see no sign of her attacker. Turning, she went through the building and out at the rear but with no success. She could see or hear nothing to tell her which way her attacker fled. As usual the rear entrance had been unfastened so that gave her no clue.

Swinging on her heel, Alice returned to the elevator. She rode to the first floor and went to her room, letting herself in with her key.

'Are you all right, Alice?' Joan asked.

'I've felt better,' Alice replied and went to the telephone. 'The other one got away, but I'll put a call out.'

After contacting Central Control and arranging for a call to be put out to all cars in her vicinity to be on the lookout for a lone woman on foot or in a car and showing signs of an injured eye, Alice turned her attention to the two attackers she and Joan managed to capture.

They lay side by side on the floor, groaning their way to consciousness. The bigger woman was a Mexican, black-haired, beautiful—or would be when not mussed up—with a magnificent body that her open coat and black sheath dress did nothing to hide. While good-looking, the other did not come up to the Mexican's standard, but was pleasant, red-haired, shapely and wore a rumpled two-piece. One reason that they lay so close together was that after dragging them into the room, Joan secured them with her handcuffs.

'Recognise them?' Joan asked.

'Inez Herrero and Kathie O'Neil,' Alice replied. 'But I never gave either of them a reason to want to jump me.'

However she had given another woman cause to want revenge earlier that day, Alice remembered. Yet it did not seem likely that Marla Blumfeld would know how to contact Inez Herrero and Kathie O'Neil.

'We'll ask them about it at the office,' Joan suggested. 'Say, you'll have quite an eye in the morning.'

'Thank you for the concern,' Alice answered. 'I'll go change.'

By the time Alice had repaired as much of the damage as possible, and changed into her uniform, she found Joan also dressed in khaki slacks and shirt. The two prisoners now sat sullenly scowling about them, but not talking.

'Did you see the other one?' Alice asked, putting on her

stadium coat.

'No,' Joan answered and picked her coat and bag up. 'She must have lammed as soon as I opened the door. Reckon this has anything to do with Tom's death?'

'I don't know. On your feet, girls, we're taking a little ride.'

The sheriff's office was empty when Alice and Joan arrived with their prisoners. After booking the girls on the desk blotter, the official log of arrests and arrested persons, the deputies took them upstairs and into the interrogation room.

To prevent abuses or false accusations, the room had been built in two sections, separated from each other by a glass, sound-proof door. The first section was small, with a couple of chairs in which witnesses could sit and watch the interview, even though unable to hear anything said.

Neither of the girls asked for a witness, so they were seated in the second room and the questioning started.

'All right,' Alice began. 'Who was she?'

'Who?' Inez replied.

'The third woman.'

'What third woman?' countered Kathie, her accent Irish.

'Don't play games with me!' Alice snapped. 'There were three of you!'

'Maybe it's you can't count, Alice,' sneered Kathie.

'Call me Alice again and we'll have a little talk alone. Who was she?'

'There were only two of us,' Kathie answered sullenly.

'Why were you waiting for Deputy Fayde?' Joan put in.

'We weren't waiting for her,' Inez replied. 'We hadn't made room-rent all night and thought we'd raise it by mugging some dame.'

'Mugging!' Joan scoffed. 'That's a laugh. You pair never did anything more serious than lifting a drunk's wallet while he rolled in the hay with you.'

'We all make a change some time,' Inez said. 'I've even heard about cops stopping taking.'

Joan smiled at Inez and started to remove her leather stadium coat. 'Just take Kathie next door, Alice. I think Inez wants to talk with me alone.'

Which was one thing Inez did not want. Every hooker in

town learned early that Joan Hilton was one female fuzz you did not fuss with.

'Look. J—Miss Hilton,' Inez yelped. 'We're levelling. Hell, do you think we'd try to mug Miss Fayde if we made her as a cop?'

'Why were you waiting in the Chadwick?' Alice put in.

'At that hour we'd've attracted attention on the streets, and we knew that a lot of unattached dames live there. We didn't chance hanging around on the ground floor and didn't want to go too high in case we had to lam.'

'How about the third woman?' asked Alice.

'Third woman!' Kathie yelled. 'What you keep bugging us with the third woman bit for?'

'Was she a blonde?' Alice went on, ignoring the outburst.

'Who?'

'How'd she know where to contact you?' Alice continued.

'We was just the two of us. T-w-o—Two!' Inez shouted. 'We was mugging, that's all, just us two.'

On the face of it, the girls might be telling the truth about their reason for being at the Chadwick; that part sounded like crook thinking. For the other, the girls might be following the underworld tradition of not squealing on a friend who had been fortunate enough to escape.

Alice knew her suspicions against Marla Blumfeld were based more on dislike than actual knowledge. Wild Marla might have been, but she never associated with prostitutes and, even though married to a retired gambler, probably could not contact Inez and Kathie to arrange for their assistance.

Before anything more could be said, the door opened and the desk sergeant entered followed by a tall, slim, well-dressed man.

'This's Mr Otis V. Caldicott, Alice. He's come to see his clients.'

'Huh?' gasped Alice.

She knew Caldicott by reputation as a trial lawyer who skidded very close to the edge of the law and often represented big-time crooks who fell into trouble. Yet while the girls were good-class hookers, they did not have the kind of money needed to retain Caldicott's services.

'I wish to see my clients alone, please,' Caldicott announced.

Much as Alice wanted to refuse, for she knew that she would never learn the third woman's identity with Caldicott present, she could not. If she tried, Caldicott would have her charged under Article 1176 of the Penal Code, refusal to allow consultation with counsel.

'We'll wait in the witnesses room,' Joan said and Alice nodded.

'Don't ask me,' said the desk sergeant, reading Alice's question before she asked it. 'He just came in, said we were holding Incz and Kathic and wanted to see them. What could I do?'

'Only what you did,' Alice answered, watching the lawyer talking with the girls beyond the door.

After a short time Caldicott came out. 'My clients wish to make statements admitting to assault with intent to rob. I want to be present for any further interviews you hold with them.'

Alice sucked in a long, angry breath. 'We'll have a stenographer up here,' she told the sergeant.

With the statements taken and signed, including a clause Alice insisted on—saying Inez and Kathie's injuries were caused during the attempted mugging and while resisting arrest—the lawyer left. Alice and Joan escorted their prisoners to the detention cells on the top floor, leaving them in the care of the night duty woman deputy.

There would be no point in questioning the girls further, with Caldicott present and ready to counter any move at learning the identity of the third woman; for Alice guessed that he arrived to do just that. She wondered what inducement the man could have given to Inez and Kathie, causing them to sign statements to their guilt under Article 1163 which carried a penalty of from two to ten years' imprisonment.

'Who was the blonde, Alice?' Joan asked.

'Just a hunch that didn't pay off,' Alice replied, leading the way to the elevator doors.

At the fourth floor, the elevator stopped, its doors opening to admit a young woman wearing police uniform.

'Hi, Alice, Joan,' she greeted. 'Say, you called asking for a general for a dame with a shiner, didn't you?'

'Sure,' Alice admitted.

'Did she give you the mouse?'

'Nope,' Alice replied, gently fingering her swollen, discoloured eye. 'I had to fight her for it.'

'How corny can you get?' sniffed Joan, then looked at the policewoman, a dispatcher on Central Control. 'Did you have anything on the general?'

'Nothing. We had to re-direct all the Upton Heights R.P.s though. There was a gun fight outside the Beverly Arms on George Terrace.'

Letting out an involuntary gasp, Alice turned her face towards Joan. Both knew that Brad Counter lived at the Beverly Arms—but had he been involved in the gun fight?

CHAPTER THIRTEEN

AFTER leaving Alice, Brad went to the Badge Diner and shared a table with Rafferty and Chu who had been answering a call. McCall joined them and over a meal the deputies kicked around Brad's case then talked about things in general. At about the time Alice left the elevator at the Chadwick Building, Brad was climbing into his M.G. to drive home.

The Beverly Arms on George Street was a large, imposing building offering comfort and pleasant surroundings to its occupants. Decorative gardens surrounded by a low wall separated the building from the streets. From the main gates, wide, bush-lined concrete paths led to the main entrance and the doors to the basement garage.

Swinging the M.G. on to George Terrace, Brad looked ahead towards the building. A few lights still showed at windows, but for the most part the occupants appeared to be in bed. Brad noticed that the lamp which usually illuminated the garage doors was out, but thought nothing about it.

Even as the M.G. came on to George Terrace, Brad saw an R.P. car cruising towards him and approaching the main gates to the building. He gave the black and white patrol car hardly more than a glance. Upton Heights was a well-policed division, but Brad knew only a few of its officers and doubted if he would be acquainted with the car's crew. Anyway, after the previous night's work he did not feel like stopping to chat.

Just as it came level with the gates, the R.P. stopped, its right side door opening and the patrolman riding shotgun leapt out. Drawing his revolver as he went, the shotgun advanced towards the gates.

Now Brad gave the car his full attention. He saw a spurt of flame stab from the bushes by the garage doors, recognising it as the muzzle-blast of a firearm even though he heard no shot. Although Brad could not be sure at that distance, he thought he saw the R.P.'s driver suddenly jerk and flop sideways.

'Not another!' he breathed. 'Not two in one week!'

Even as the words came, Brad gave a thought to assisting his fellow officers. Yet he was also aware of the danger he faced cutting in on the trouble without first notifying the policemen that he had the right as another peace officer. The patrolmen probably did not know him; his M.G. carried civilian licence plates; he did not even wear his deputy's uniform. So he must give some sign of his official position before butting in and helping.

Slowing the M.G., he reached into his inside pocket, drew out the ID wallet and extracted the deputy's badge, slipping its hook into his buttonhole. From what Brad saw while doing this, he felt pleased that he took the precaution.

On the shot from the garage doors, the patrolman at the gate swivelled his head towards the R.P., then turned again. After that he moved fast and proved the wisdom Brad had shown in taking precautions. Swiftly the patrolman dropped into the braced kneeling position, right knee on the ground, left elbow on raised left knee as its hand supported the extended right arm. It was a position offering good support for the gun and a steady platform from which to take careful aim when shooting at distances of seventy or more yards. If Brad had joined the fight unannounced, a man so skilled in combat shooting was capable of making the deputy regret his hasty action.

Two more shots hammered from the bushes as the patrolman dropped into his position. Taking aim at the dark shape from which the shots came, he sent a bullet in return. Even as his heavy calibre revolver bucked in his palm, he saw the shape rock under the impact of lead, stagger and fall. Before he could take further action, the patrolman's attention was drawn to further along the street.

After hooking on his badge, Brad brought the M.G. to a halt. From what he had seen, the patrolman knew enough about guns not to panic or shoot without making sure he threw lead at an enemy. So Brad thrust open the door of his car. The imported vehicle's right hand drive brought him on to the sidewalk as he quit the steering wheel. He stepped out and into trouble.

A movement in the bushes beyond the wall caught his eye. Turning to check on whatever attracted his attention, he saw a splash of white where no such colour should be. Swiftly Brad straightened up, yet even so it seemed he might be too late.

Wearing a black leather jacket, open to show the white T-shirt which gave his position away, a tall, slim young man bounded the garden wall. He landed not twenty feet from where Brad stood, the short barrelled revolver in his hand slanting towards the deputy, belching flame as he fired at the big blond—and missed.

Brad heard the flat 'splat' of a close-passing bullet. Instantly his brain snapped an order that put his trained reactions into operation. In one smoothly co-ordinated blur of movement, Brad's left hand gripped and drew open the side of his jacket to leave the way clear for his right hand which already rose and went across towards the butt of his automatic. At the same time he threw his weight forward on to the balls of his feet, facing the man on slightly bent legs and with his spine slanting forward. The Colt pivoted from the spring clips of the holster, swinging around until Brad's right elbow was about eight inches ahead of his right hip, pointing the automatic's bore straight towards the man. Even in the emotional strain of being under fire, Brad did not thumb down the manual safety catch or place his finger upon the trigger until the gun's muzzle lined away from him.

For all that, the instant the Colt lined on the man—·6 of a second after Brad's brain gave its order—the deputy fired his first shot.

With the young man facing and shooting at him, Brad did not have time to adopt any fancy shoulder-high, sideways to the target position. Nor did he need to do so at close range. Instead he went into the instinctive-alignment combat crouch devised by the F.B.I. for use on such occasions. It was the short-range, maximum speed fighting position, useless when an enemy beyond about seven yards, but deadly effective up to that range when performed by a master.

The young man from the garden stood just within the seven yards range. After his first shot missed, he triggered off a second which came so close that Brad felt a quick tug at his jacket sleeve. Although the man was swinging his gun towards Brad in an attempt to correct his aim, he touched off the shot an instant too soon. He fired his second shot almost as a reflex action to the first. Brad knew from the way the revolver moved, the next shot would hit him.

Only the next shot fired came from Brad's gun. The big automatic roared, its slide kicked back, ejecting an empty case and rode forward to feed another bullet into the chamber. Again Brad's finger squeezed the trigger, but not as a wild reflex action. He checked the recoil's kick, wrist locked rigid and acting as an extension of his eyes, keeping the automatic's barrel pointed at the target and sending off another *aimed* shot.

Struck in the chest by two .45 bullets, the young man was thrown backwards. His revolver fell from his hand as his legs struck the wall and he fell back into the garden. Even as the man started to go down, Brad saw two spreading dark stains on the white of the T-shirt's left breast.

Brad stood still for a moment, fighting down the revulsion which rose at his having to shoot at another human being. Yet he kept his automatic lined and ready for use, aimed at where a pair of motor-cycle boots rose into the air from beyond the garden wall.

A television western or detective hero faced with Brad's problem would have blown the revolver out of the man's hand with a well-placed shot; but Brad knew that such shooting did not exist beyond the walls of a film production lot. No man, even a master like Brad, could shoot the gun out of an enemy's hand in the heat of a fight except by pure blind luck. Under the circumstances Brad had no choice but to shoot for effect, to knock the other man down before he could fire again, for the next shot would have hit him.

If Brad had been using a lesser weapon than the .45 Colt Government Model automatic pistol, say a .38 Special snub-nosed revolver such as many a detective was forced by his departmental regulations to carry, the young man would have kept his feet long enough to send out another bullet. Brad's insistence on putting up with carrying the automatic's thirty-nine ounce weight on his person had been completely justified in that the gun saved his life.

Although aware of the shooting along the street, Brad had seen nothing of it, for his full attention had centred on his own affairs.

'Hold it!' yelled a voice as Brad started to move towards the wall. Turning, the deputy saw that the patrolman faced towards him, still in the braced kneeling position and covering him while continuing, 'Turn it and shout!'

Brad did not blame the man for taking such a precaution. Allowing his automatic to pivot around on his triggerfinger, so that the slide hung downwards and the muzzle pointed away from the R.P., he turned slowly so that the patrolman could see the badge on his lapel.

'Counter, deputy sheriff!' he called back.

The sight of the badge and the fact that Brad clearly understood the order convinced the patrolman that he dealt with a *bona fide* member of the sheriff's office, so he could relax and leave the handling of that part of the affair in capable hands.

'Check that one, sir,' the patrolman called. 'I hit the other, but he winged my partner.'

'Get him bad?' asked Brad.

'Not if his language's anything to go on.'

With that the patrolman swung away from Brad, rose and walked into the Beverly Arms' grounds. Brad returned his automatic to the firing position and moved cautiously towards the wall. All the time he kept his attention on the pair of boots which rose so incongruously into view. Lights began to appear at windows in the Beverly Arms and surrounding buildings, and Brad wanted to make sure the man he shot could not make trouble should people begin to gather.

Even as Brad swung himself over the wall, he heard the wail of sirens from four different directions and knew cars would be speeding towards George Terrace in answer either to a call from the driver of the R.P., or telephoned complaints from people in the vicinity.

Brad ignored the sound and stood for a moment looking down at the body. Taking out his lighter, he flicked the wheel and used its flame to examine the man he shot. On being struck by the bullets and thrown backwards, the man had dropped his gun and lay with empty hands. Brad needed only one quick glance to know his attacker was dead.

Shaking out the lighter, Brad returned it to his pocket, then holstered the Colt. Then he stood still for a moment. Taking another human being's life did not come easy, nor was it a thing lightly cast off. The shape on the ground looked to be around twenty, with a sallow face, long hair and the dress of a motor-cycle set member, one of the kind who hovered on the fringe of the underworld and did no work. Maybe he might have developed into a useful citizen, although few of his kind ever did. More likely that still shape on the ground would have gone on even deeper into a life of crime; and not brilliantly thought-out crime, but the type which relied upon brute force and violence to carry it through. Probably Brad had done no more than bring forward the young man's death at the hands of the law—but the thought made the deputy feel no better.

Seeing he could do nothing, Brad left the body lie as it fell. He turned, stepped over the wall and walked along the street towards the R.P. car. On his arrival, he found the driver leaning against the car's door, seated using the microphone to send out a request for an ambulance.

'How is it?' Brad asked, waiting for the man to finish.

'Hurts like hell,' the driver replied. 'Nicked the back of my neck. Just my lousy luck, I was due to start vacation next week. You'll get plenty of help here soon. This's a quiet division, we don't get much excitement. Everybody'll want to get into the act.'

The patrolman guessed correctly. Even as he finished speaking, the first of a quartet of supporting R.P. cars arrived on the scene. Brad left the wounded man to give his orders to the newcomers. First he sent the shotgun to attend to the wounded driver, then told the other member of the crew to keep everybody back from where his victim lay on the ground. As each car arrived, Brad set its crew to work, having the patrolman attend to holding back such citizens as chose to come out and investigate the cause of the shooting.

With the basic duties attended to, Brad walked along the path. He ignored the questions thrown his way by various residents and left one of his men to prevent the people following him. Going to the side of the garage, he switched on the light over its doors. The patrolman knelt by a bleeding, still form which sprawled on its back among the bushes. Although shorter and stockier than Brad's attacker, this one also bore the signs of belonging to the motor-cycle set and a Webley revolver lay just ahead of him.

'Can't do much for him,' the patrolman said, looking over his shoulder and trying to stop the bleeding, then he recognised the big deputy. 'Hi, Brad. Clean forgot you cut in.'

Recognition was mutual. Brad knew the patrolman to be another combat shooting enthusiast.

'The meat wagon's coming, Dex,' he said. 'What happened?'

'We were cruising our watch when we saw the light was out. There's been a few muggings up this way with the punks waiting for somebody to come home, then jump the victim as he gets out to open the garage doors. So the supers leave the lights on and if we see one out, we investigate. Afore I reached the gate, this punk started to throw lead. Missed me, and caught Starkey. Say, is he all right?'

'Just nicked.'

'Thought so. I heard him cursing pretty rough, that Starkey's sure got an educated tongue.'

Relief showed in Dex's voice for he and his partner were good friends.

An ambulance and a black D car arrived almost at the same time. While the car joined the police vehicles on the street, the ambulance entered the grounds and cruised to where Brad and Dex stood waiting. A white-coated M.E. jumped out and went to the wounded man, dropping to a knee beside him. Down by the gates, three men in civilian clothes climbed from the D car, one of them carrying a couple of cameras.

'That's Catlan,' Dex remarked, jerking a thumb towards the tall man who spoke to the cameraman, pointing along the street. 'Best go see him.'

'Reckon so,' Brad agreed.

'Hi, Brad,' greeted Lieutenant Catlan as the deputy walked up. 'I thought that was your heap down the street. How come you're mixed up in this?'

'Just fortunate, I reckon,' Brad replied.

'What happened, Dex?' the lieutenant went on.

Quickly Dex told Catlan the story he gave Brad, finishing

with, 'Then the punk cut loose. Must have been lucky, he caught old Starkey there first crack. Hey, Starkey, you was real lucky he was only using one of them imported Webley .38s, or he might have hurt you.'

'I got news for you,' Starkey replied. 'He *did* hurt me.'

'G'wan!' scoffed Dex. 'You can't hurt anybody with less than a .357 magnum.'

Like Brad, Dex was a firm believer in the value of a heavy calibre handgun for defence purposes, although Brad felt the patrolman could not reach his full potential as a combat shot while he insisted on carrying a Smith & Wesson Model 21 .44 Special revolver. However, in the face of the evidence just seen, Dex had no cause to complain about the effectiveness of his choice.

'If that punk hadn't been wearing a white T-shirt and his coat open, he'd've been harder to see,' Dex went on. 'I saw the splash of colour in the muzzle-blast.'

'Reckon their luck was out all the way through,' Catlan answered. 'Even if you hadn't seen them, they'd've jumped Brad as their victim.'

'Sure pleased you came along, Dex,' Brad stated. 'I've had a rough few hours and didn't want to do anything but hit the sack. Say, Bill, reckon I can go on in now? I'll turn my report in tomorrow morning.'

'Sure, Brad,' Catlan agreed. 'Say, how's it going about T——'

The words trailed off as Catlan stared down at Brad's left sleeve. Following the direction of the other's startled gaze, Brad saw that the jacket's material had a gash in it. The young crook's second bullet came so close that it slashed through the under side of the sleeve, between Brad's arm and side, in passing and without his being aware of just how close his escape from injury had been.

'Ruined a genuine Harris tweed jacket,' Brad said slowly.

'You must live right,' breathed Catlan. 'We'll get the photographer to take a couple of shots of that gash. Just in case the *Mirror* starts its trigger-happy cop bit over the shootings.'

'Be best,' Brad agreed. 'Although I should've maybe let him hit me twice before I shot back, so's to prove that my life might be in danger.'

'Don't sound all bitter, there's folks worse off than you,' Catlan grinned. 'I've a cousin working in P.R. He has to deal with the *Mirror* staff. Office never smells the same for days after they've been.'

After taking the elementary precautions against abuses by the liberal-intellectual press, Brad collected his car and drove to the garage. Already the photographer had done his work there and the wounded crook was placed in the ambulance. Once a way was cleared, Brad drove the M.G. into the basement garage and parked it. He rode the elevator to the second floor and went to his apartment. Inside he cleaned his gun, changed the loads in his magazines, leaving the ones used that day empty to prevent metal fatigue ruining the feed springs, and reloaded spares. While that might strike some people as a lot of trouble, Brad did not regard it as such. The extra few minutes taken to rotate magazines could mean the continuance or failure of correct operation of his gun—and that meant the difference between life and death when a peace officer needed his weapon to save himself.

Brad slept late the following morning. Rising, he took a shower, shaved and then cooked breakfast. While reading an account of the gun fight in the *Daily Lightning*, a thought struck Brad. The same thought had nagged him the previous night but he was too tired to examine it fully. Putting aside the paper, he rose and went to the telephone, dialled the office's number and asked to speak with Joan Hilton.

'We heard about it last night,' Joan said when he mentioned the shooting.

'How come?' Brad asked.

'Looks like mugging the law was in favour,' Joan explained. 'There were three gals waiting at the Chadwick Building and they hit Alice. We nailed two and the third got away. Then when we brought our catch in, Alice heard about the shooting at the Beverly Arms and stayed on until she heard you were all right. Have you tried calling her?'

'I don't know her home number.'

'It's Lasher 7630.'

Hanging up, Brad dialled Alice's number and let the phone at the other end ring for a time without result. Knowing that the girl kept her telephone in whichever room she was using,

Brad decided Alice could not be at her apartment. He hung up his receiver for a moment, then took it off the hook again and called the office.

'She's not at home, Joan,' he said. 'Any idea where she might be?'

'No, she didn't call in and tell us,' Joan replied. 'She may have gone out to try to find that blonde she kept asking about last night.'

A cold sensation hit Brad as he stared down into the mouth of the receiver. 'What blonde was that?' he asked.

Sensing the worry in Brad's voice, Joan told him everything that happened the previous night, including Alice's questions about the third member of the attacking party.

'It sounded like Alice knew the third one,' Joan continued. 'Only before we could work on it, Caldicott arrived and queered our pitch.'

After hearing about Caldicott's intervention, Brad felt even more certain that the two punks had not been waiting outside the Beverly Arms by chance. The feeling, nagging him since he got out of bed, grew more and more as he realised the implications behind the two attacks. Neither of the shot men had been Rosenthal, but looked the kind of company he would keep.

'Check on those two punks for me, Joan,' he said. 'Try for a tie-in with Benny Rosenthal. Ask Craddock at R. and I. for details of Rosenthal's past.'

'I'll see to it, Brad,' Joan promised. 'What's up?'

'Just a hunch, Joan. Don't try to reach me here. I'm hitting the streets and don't know when I'll be back. I'll call in as often as I can.'

'Sure, Brad,' Joan answered.

Brad put down the telephone and crossed the room. Strapping on his holster, he took up the gun, fed a magazine into the butt slot, jerked the cocking-slide to load a bullet into the chamber, set on the manual safety and slid the weapon into the holster. At the wardrobe he took out an undamaged jacket. Placing two loaded magazines into the special pocket built into the left side lining of the jacket, he left his apartment and rode the elevator to the basement.

Collecting his car, Brad drove through the streets of Upton Heights, winding higher until he reached Beunavista Avenue. He hoped he would reach the Blumfeld house before Alice arrived and confronted Marla.

CHAPTER FOURTEEN

ALICE FAYDE slept restlessly and fitfully all night. Ever since hearing of the gun fight outside the Beverly Arms, she felt sure that Marla Blumfeld had been responsible for the attack on herself and the presence of the two punks at Brad's place. Having met Rosenthal, Alice doubted if he had stayed on the straight since his last term in prison and guessed that he still retained his old contacts. Rosenthal could gather the necessary help to make a try at Brad, might even have known how to contact Inez and Kathie; and Marla's money would meet Caldicott's fees.

Yet Alice wondered what prompted the attacks. Certainly Rosenthal met with rough handling when he hit Brad, but the young chauffeur would have more sense than jump a peace officer for that, especially so soon after the event, when he would be the first suspect for the attack. Nor did she think that Marla would go to such extremes merely because Alice caught and twisted her arm—even though Alice knew she did use more force than absolutely necessary. The old hate between them still existed, but Marla would not jeopardise her future merely to take revenge on an old rival.

In her restless frame of mind, tired and with her body aching from the beating taken the previous night, Alice clean forgot the speech Brad made on leaving Marla's presence.

At nine o'clock Alice rose and prepared to go out. She drove downtown to a Turkish bath-house where she went through the full treatment, finally laying naked on a bench while a plump, red haired, jovial masseuse worked the throb and ache out of her tormented bones.

'They sure worked you over good, Alice,' said the masseuse cheerily as her strong fingers dug skilfully into the girl's flesh.

'That's some shiner you have.'

'You should see the other guy,' Alice replied, feeling better already although no less emotionally disturbed. 'What do you know about Inez Herrero and Kathie O'Neil, Anna?'

The question did not appear to surprise the masseuse, although she glanced around the deserted massage room before answering.

'Hookers. Handle a good class of trade. All upper-middle-class and above customers. Tough cookies. Did they——?'

'Sure, only I want to know why they jumped me. Are they friends?'

Not only did Alice visit the baths for a refresher, but also to see the masseuse who was an informer with almost encyclopaedic knowledge of the female side of the Gusher City underworld.

'Not buddy-buddy share-the-same-apartment friends,' the masseuse answered. 'They both deal with the same type of trade, but don't cut in on each other's territory. I wouldn't say they were close friends.'

'How much do you know about their backgrounds?'

'You mean when they're not on the streets?'

'Sure, home life; like that.'

Anna thought for a moment before replying, 'Kathie supports her old man. He was a safe-popper, a good one, until he goofed on a blow-job and killed two of his mob. When he came out of the Walls his nerve had gone. He's an old rum-head now and Kathie works hard to keep him.'

'And Inez?' asked Alice.

'Off the streets she's clean. Lives in the Mexican section of Greevers. Has a nice little place. Just her, her mother—and daughter.'

'Daughter?' Alice repeated, knowing from the slight pause that there must be more to the words than a mere list of house occupants.

'Kid's maybe six now, doesn't know what her mother works at at nights and Inez would kill anybody who told her. She lives for that kid, takes her to church on Sundays, gives her everything money can buy. I've seen Inez uptown with the kid at a rodeo and nearly didn't recognise her. No make-up, hair took back in a bun, glasses, a dress that hid her shape;

which takes some doing. None of her regular customers would have known her if they passed her in good light. Yes sir, Inez's a real good mother to that kid. Does that help you any?'

'It may. Get me a telephone please, Anna, I want to make some calls.'

Dialling the Vice and Gambling Detail's number, Alice reached one of her friends and asked for the two hookers' home addresses. By the time she had received the full massage and dressed, the V. and G. detective called back and gave her the information she required. Alice paid for her course of treatment and the information received, then, feeling much refreshed, left the bath-house.

First she drove to Kathie O'Neil's home address, an apartment building in the Evans Park section of the Bad-Bit. The area was slightly better quality than most of the Bad-Bit and its occupants not such confirmed cop-haters as most of the citizens who lived in the slum district. However, Alice expected a certain amount of objection to answering her questions.

Much to her surprise, the building's superintendent talked freely, expressing wonder at the events of the morning. A well-dressed man visited Seamus O'Neil earlier and talked with the old man. Before leaving, the visitor came to the super's office and paid one year's rent in advance for the O'Neil apartment. As soon as the visitor left, O'Neil came downstairs in a hurry, showing great excitement, and headed for the bar across the street.

Parrying the superintendent's questions as to the reason for her visit, Alice left the building and crossed the street to the bar. Looking in through the window, she saw an old man seated on the counter, whiskey bottle in hand, entertaining a bunch of his cronies to drinks and cigars.

'And only last night he wanted to borrow a dollar off me for beer,' said the super's voice at Alice's elbow. 'Say, I just thought after you left. That feller who come here, he asked me how to get to Salvador Street.'

Alice swung to look at the man, knowing that Inez Herrero lived on Salvador Street. 'Thanks,' she said, and looked for an official telephone.

Finding what she sought, Alice put in a call to the local

station house and then drove her Mustang through the streets. On reaching her destination, she found a D car waiting some distance below the Herrero house. However, a Chevrolet coupé stood before the building and even as Alice drove up, she saw a man enter it.

'Tail him,' she said to the male detective, showing her ID wallet. 'Get his number if nothing else.'

'Can do,' the man replied.

Jumping out, the female detective watched the D car cruise away, then she turned to Alice.

'What now?' she asked.

'We'll go and see Mrs Herrero.'

Salvador Street was one of the better sections of Greevers and the Herrero house a small, neat, well-kept building which showed loving care. A short, plump Mexican woman opened the door to Alice's ring and studied the callers. Although both wore civilian clothes and the local detective was of Mexican birth, Mrs Herrero made them immediately as peace officers.

'What do you want?' she asked worriedly, glancing at the tell-tale handbags. 'You're the police.'

'Yes, Mrs Herrero,' agreed Alice, rather than become involved in a discussion about the difference between police and sheriff's office personnel.

'Then the man lied.'

'About what, Mrs Herrero?' Alice said.

'About the mon——' the woman began, then stopped and looked at Alice's discoloured eye. 'Are you the one who arrested Inez?'

Alice did not have a chance to reply. A pretty little girl, her hair in braids and wearing a clean dress, appeared at the door, wriggling by her grandmother and smiling up at the two peace officers.

'Oh!' she said, sounding disappointed. 'I thought it was Mommy. Are you her friends? Will you be going on vacation with her? Will she be coming home to kiss me goodbye before she leaves?'

For once in her life Alice could not think of a thing to say. Words just would not come as she looked down at the pretty little child whose mother was a prostitute and probably never knew her father's identity. Clearly the child loved her mother, but would be unlikely to see Inez again for at least five years.

Alice felt anger welling up inside her. Deep and bitter hatred formed against the woman who hired Inez Herrero, deserted her when the going grew tough and bought her silence by offering to support her daughter while she was in prison.

It might be argued that the child would fare better without such a mother. But, for all her faults, Inez Herrero loved that child and cared enough for her well-being to accept a long term in the Goree Unit of the Texas Prison System as long as money would be sent to her daughter.

'Go back into the house, Maria,' Mrs Herrero said gently. 'Say goodbye to the ladies.'

'Goodbye,' the girl complied. 'If you see Mommy and she can't come home before she leaves on vacation, tell her my love and ask her to write to me as soon as she can.'

Alice gulped, trying to clear something which seemed to block her throat. No words came as the little girl turned and walked back into the house. Then Alice let out a long sigh.

'Why did Inez do it?' Mrs Herrero asked. 'She had a good place, brought home money. Why did she attack you?'

'How did you know about that?' Alice inquired.

'I made the man tell me, before I signed the letter he brought and took his cheque. He said she and another girl went mugging and were caught when they picked on a detective. Only Inez wasn't a mugger. Oh, I know how she made her money, but she never stole a dime in her life.'

'Was she in any financial difficulties, Mrs Herrero?' asked the detective.

'Things aren't easy, keeping this house going and her place in Central, but she didn't need money bad enough to go mugging to get it.'

'Who was the man?' Alice put in.

'He works for some bonding agency downtown,' answered Mrs Herrero. 'But why did my little Inez go wrong?'

'We don't know, Mrs Herrero,' Alice answered. 'How much money did he give you?'

'A thousand dollars and he said he would send me a cheque for another thousand for each year Inez drew in her sentence.'

'And that could run into money,' remarked the detective as they left the Herrero place. 'She'll pull five at least.'

'At least,' Alice agreed bitterly.

'You're not sorry for her, are you?' asked the detective, glancing pointedly at Alice's bruised face.

'Not for her, for the kid,' Alice snapped.

'Did you learn what you wanted?'

A long, shuddering sigh left Alice's lips. 'I learned enough.'

After driving the detective back to her station house, Alice returned to the Chadwick Building. In her apartment she changed from her smart two-piece to a dark blue blouse and a pair of stretch pants. For the first time since joining the G.C.P.D., Alice intended to break the rules, go against everything she had been taught and forget that she was a peace officer. With that thought in mind, she left her handbag on the chair. If she must break the rules, then she did not intend to take along anything to officially identify her with the county's law-enforcement authorities.

In cold, deadly anger she drove across town, into Upton Heights and brought her car to a halt before the Blumfeld mansion. Climbing out, she looked around her. There was no sign of either of the cars and Rosenthal did not appear to be around. Just as Alice walked towards the main doors, she caught a movement to her right. Turning, she saw Marla step out of a french window. The blonde wore a figure-hugging white sharkskin swimsuit of daring cut, carried a towel in one hand and a pair of dark glasses in the other.

Even as Alice saw Marla, the blonde looked her way. Quickly Marla whipped up the glasses, slipping them on. Then she stood arrogantly watching Alice walk towards her. Although aware of it, Alice ignored the sensual physical attraction of Marla's magnificent body, her attention being on the other's left hand. The big diamond cluster ring had gone. Lifting her eyes to Marla's face, Alice saw that make-up could not hide the swollen and discoloured condition of the blonde's right eye.

'Hello, Marla, or do I have to call you Mrs Blumfeld?'

Throwing a startled glance first at Alice then towards the upstairs windows, Marla let the towel fall to the ground, then backed into the house. Alice followed and found herself in the sitting-room where she met Marla the previous day. It looked much the same, except that the whiskey decanter and glasses had gone and the ashtray was wiped clean. Not until they stood in the centre of the room did Marla halt or offer to speak.

'What do you want here?' she asked.

'Where'd you get the mouse?' Alice replied.

'Mouse?' Marla repeated, raising a hand to touch her right eye. The gold wedding band glowed coldly and the diamond ring had left a faint white line on the tanned skin. 'I walked into a door.'

'At the Chadwick Building?'

'Slumming for kicks went out years ago in my set, darling,' Marla purred. 'The in thing now is——'

'Where'd you get it, Marla?' Alice snapped.

'Why, right here, at home. Last night at around half past eleven. I'm sure Weems will bear me out on that.'

'I'm sure he will,' Alice agreed. 'By the way, where's your chauffeur?'

Cold anger, suspicion and a hint of fear warred on Marla's face and she paused for a time before answering, 'He's gone downtown on a job.'

'When will he be back?'

'Oh, how should I know? Ask Weems.'

'Weems seems to know everything that happens around here,' Alice commented. 'Does he know where you lost your diamond ring?'

Marla dropped her eyes to the left hand, then jerked them back to face Alice once more. 'I don't wear it when I'm going swimming.'

'What would that ring fetch?' Alice asked. 'Five grand, seventy-five hundred?'

'It's worth twenty thousand,' Marla answered. 'Which's why I don't wear——'

'But that would be on the open market, wouldn't it,' Alice interrupted. 'Not as a quick sale and through the channels needed to get rid of it.'

'And what does that mean?'

'Your husband's probably generous with your allowance, but laying hands on enough to grease Caldicott and the two hookers would take some finding.'

'I don't know what you mean,' Marla said, 'but I think I'd better call my husband.'

'Go right ahead,' Alice replied, waving a hand towards the telephone.

Despite Alice's invitation, Marla made no move to call her husband. Cold fury twisted her beautiful face and her right hand quivered as she raised it to point to the door.

'Get out of here, Alice Fayde!' she ordered.

'Not until I'm ready,' Alice answered. 'Last night you and two hookers were waiting for me at the Chadwick Building. That's where you got that shiner. I gave it to you before you turned and ran out on the girls you brought along to help you do your dirty work.'

'And can you prove that?' asked Marla, a hint of mocking triumph in her voice and a sneer flickering on her lips.

'We have the girls at Headquarters.'

Alice's bluff failed as much as did Marla's when the blonde threatened to call her husband.

'Then you can prove what you're saying, can't you?'

'You know I can't,' Alice admitted. 'Caldicott picked girls who needed money and under certain conditions would be willing to keep quiet if things went wrong. They went wrong and we caught Inez and Kathie. Only he arrived at the office, called out by you, and settled the details with the girls. They keep quiet and you support their dependants while they're in the Goree Unit.'

'Which of course you can prove,' purred Marla.

'You know I can't. Caldicott covered his tracks too well and your house staff will tell any lie you want telling.'

'Then stop wasting my time and get out of here, *cop*!'

Alice's scorn showed plain as she looked Marla up and down. 'You haven't changed, Marla. You're still the same cheap, vicious little tramp I knew. The cheap little slut with the big ideas. A dirty, nasty little hooker who married rich and cheated on her husband——'

Which was when Marla hit her.

CHAPTER FIFTEEN

Knotting her right hand into a fist, Marla swung it around in a full-blooded drive that ended at the side of Alice's cheek. Although Alice knew her words would goad Marla into an attack, she had not expected it to come with such speed or power. The blow snapped Alice's head to one side and staggered her backwards a few paces. Even as she caught her balance, Alice saw Marla leaping at her with greedy fingers reaching for hair.

With her training and physical fitness, Alice ought to have been able to take Marla with ease. Yet the moment Marla's fingers dug into red hair and tore at it, every lesson Alice received in self-defence tactics left her. Up drove her hands to sink into Marla's hair, digging deep and pulling.

Clinging to each other's hair, tearing and shaking at it, the girls staggered up and down the room. Their feet hacked at each other's shins, gasps of pain and squeals of fury left their lips. Suddenly Marla released her hold, placed her hands against Alice's body and shoved hard. Alice lost her hold and went sprawling into the wall. Bouncing forward, she landed a slap that left finger marks on Marla's cheek and whipped across a punch that jolted the blonde's head back in the other direction. Marla responded in the same manner, fists and flat hands lashing out, landing on Alice's face and shoulders, blindly impervious to the blows and slaps raining on her.

Once again they closed, grabbing hair with one hand, striking, gripping and pushing with the other. More by accident than design Marla hooked a leg behind Alice and they went down still locked in each other's grasp. Over and over they churned on the floor in a wild, unskilled wrestling tangle. For almost four minutes they rolled and struggled, going on to the divan and bouncing back to the floor. Alice lost her shoes and the criss-cross fastenings of Marla's left Grecian slipper came unfastened, falling from her wildly waving, shapely leg. Buttons popped from Alice's blouse and it ripped along one shoulder. She felt the material tangling her arms and wriggled the arms free, leaving the blouse trailing down her back. Soon after Alice's widely clawing fingers ripped the right shoulder strap from Marla's swimsuit, yet so blindly furious were they that neither girl gave a thought to the damage their clothing suffered.

So filled with blind rage were the girls, that they might have gone on rolling and tearing at each other until exhaustion brought an end to the brawl. They bit, hit, kicked, locked legs around each other, screaming, gasping and mouthing curses. Then Marla burrowed her head down and bit hard, her teeth sinking into the bare flesh just under Alice's breasts. Burning pain knifed into Alice and jolted her out of the fight-rage which filled her. Suddenly she realised what she was doing and also that she must end this madness before one of them received a serious injury.

All this tore through Alice's mind as she screeched in pain and hurled the blonde away from her. Blood oozed out of the bite, a deep oval of indentations in her flesh. Marla landed on her back, once elegant hair looking like a tangled wool mop, face reddened, sweat and tear-soaked, the make-up smeared and marred by blood. In the struggle the swimsuit had torn away from her right side and a bare breast showed brown against the white material—it seemed that Marla sun-bathed in the nude to obtain an all-over tan. The tanned flesh showed bruises where Alice's fists landed, fingers dug in or the blonde crashed into furniture.

The sight shocked Alice, even though a glance in the mirror would have shown her that she looked in little better shape.

'Marla!' she gasped, starting to rise and feeling her bra hang loose, its fastener burst open at some stage of the fight. 'Cut it——'

Mouthing curses, Marla flung herself forward. Only now she attacked a trained peace officer, one who knew how to handle such a situation. Still on her knees, Alice lashed around a right fist, catching Marla's jaw and knocking the blonde sideways across the room.

Marla landed hard, rolling over, yet she came up and rushed forward again. Stepping in, Alice ripped her left fist into Marla's belly. A moan left the blonde's lips as her hand clutched at her middle and she doubled over. On the heels of the belly blow, Alice brought up her knee, driving it into the down-dropping face. Fortunately for Marla, she had gone back a step on being hit, so the knee hit her forehead instead of landing on her nose. The force of the attack still lifted Marla erect and Alice swung a roundhouse left. Pain and numbness knifed into Alice as her fist smashed into the side of Marla's jaw. The blow snapped the blonde head to one side and sent Marla sprawling on to the divan, where she hung limp and still.

Staggering in exhaustion, Alice almost fell. She stumbled towards the door just as it burst open. Weems, a furious-looking, well-dressed big man and a couple of maids crowded forward into the room.

'What the hell?' the big man roared, staring from Alice to Marla. 'Grab her, you women. Weems, go call an ambulance, Doctor Hosewith and the cops!'

Her breath coming in saw-rasping grunts, Alice could not speak and she felt too exhausted to resist as the two maids caught her by the arms. Suddenly she realised her position and knew that her career as a peace officer would most likely be at an end.

Before Weems could obey his employer's order, the door bell chimed. Crossing the hall and opening the door, Weems found himself face to face with Brad Counter. The big deputy took one look at Weems, then through the door of the sitting-room.

An angry growl left Brad's lips at what he saw. He swept by the butler and across the hall, making for the sitting-room. A cold, sinking feeling drove into the big deputy's belly as he saw the battered Alice held by the maids. It seemed that he had reached the Blumfeld place too late.

'Who the hell're you?' growled Blumfeld as Brad entered the room.

'Counter, deputy sheriff.'

'I don't know how the hell you got here so quick,' Blumfeld

barked and pointed a finger at Alice. 'That frail bust in here and attacked my wife. Take her in.'

Ignoring the man, Brad looked at Alice. 'What started it?'

'I just told you!' Blumfeld bellowed. 'Take her——'

'What started it, Alice?' Brad repeated.

'You know her?' barked Blumfeld.

'She's my partner,' Brad replied.

Being a professional gambler taught a man to control his emotions, but Blumfeld's normally expressionless face showed surprise and anger as he glared from Brad to Alice and then back again.

'She's your——'

'Suppose we have the women-folks see to their hurts first,' Brad interrupted.

While Brad's words might not have brought any effect, a groan from Marla caused Blumfeld to snap an order. The two maids released Alice and she fell into a chair. Reaction set in and she began to sob, her hands pulling the blouse together in a belated attempt to hide her half-naked condition.

Brad could see that Alice was in no serious danger and so turned his attention to where the maids had rolled Marla on to her back upon the divan. One of the women darted from the room and returned with a first-aid box. Showing considerable knowledge of handling fight injuries, the maids started to work on Marla. Not until sure his wife would be all right did Blumfeld turn from her. He strode across the room and stood glaring at Brad and Alice.

'I don't give a damn who she is,' he snarled. 'I want her taken in for assaulting my wife.'

'Not until I hear who and what started the fight,' Brad answered.

'Weems!' Blumfeld barked. 'Go call my lawyer.'

'And while you're at it, Weems,' Brad put in before the butler could move, 'call Howard Thirston at his office, ask him to come over.'

'Thirston?' grunted Blumfeld, knowing that to be the name of one of the shrewdest lawyers in Texas.

'He handles my family's affairs down here and I figure Miss Fayde needs legal representation in this matter,' Brad answered calmly.

Blumfeld watched Brad with a gambler's eyes and read no hint that the big deputy might be trying a bluff. Studying Brad's clothing, Blumfeld estimated their value and knew that such an outfit cost far more than a deputy living on his salary could afford. Blumfeld knew also that the control of Rockabye County's law-enforcement organisation was such that no officer could make enough in graft to clothe himself so well and remain undetected. Finally, the name Counter meant something to Blumfeld and he did not doubt that Brad could call on Thirston's services.

'All right,' Blumfeld said defiantly. 'Call your lawyer.'

Thrusting the maids' hands from her, Marla sat stiffly up and said, 'Stan!'

'Yes, honey?'

'There's no need to talk of sending for lawyers. Alice and I are old friends and she came to visit me. You know I've been learning judo? Well she offered to teach me a few throws. I landed awkwardly and lost my temper. When I grabbed hair, Alice lost her's too and we tangled. But it wasn't anybody's fault.'

For a moment Alice stared at Marla, their eyes locking. Alice knew that Marla did not speak out of charitable motives, or because her conscience troubled her. Being aware of how much Alice's career meant to her, Marla took a more subtle revenge than sending the deputy before the Commissioners' Disciplinary Board to be broken. For the rest of her life Alice would know she owed her position to Marla.

'It's a l——!' Alice began.

Brad swung towards her, his face set and hard. 'Go out and wait in my car!' he ordered, and as the girl hesitated went on, 'Do it, damn you, Alice, or I'll——'

The words trailed off and Alice saw his right hand quivering. At any moment she expected to feel his palm lash across her face and knew why. Like Alice, Brad was a career peace officer. His whole career hung in the balance and she knew that he staked it to dig her out of a jam *her* momentary foolishness brought her into. Instead of helping, she tried to state that Marla lied. Slowly she turned and walked out of the room. Brad watched her go before turning to Blumfeld.

'Do you accept your wife's explanation, sir?'

'If that's the way she wants it.'

'It is, Stan,' Marla stated.

'Then that's the way it is!' grunted Blumfeld.

'I'd like to see your chauffeur before I leave, sir,' Brad said.

'Why?' Blumfeld asked. 'And don't give me that "just routine" bit.'

'Last night three young men were waiting for me outside the Beverly Arms and I've reason to believe that Rosenthal was one of them. Don't trouble to ask me why I believe it, but I've strong enough reasons and want to see him.'

'Where is he, Weems?' Blumfeld inquired.

'He returned from town somewhat hurriedly last night, sir,' the butler answered. 'I heard him drive off again soon after. On looking into his room this morning I discovered all his belongings had gone, as is his private car.'

'Why didn't you——' Blumfeld began.

'What make of car, Weems?' Brad interrupted.

'A '58 Dodge hardtop, sir. Light grey in colour. I'm afraid I don't know the number,' Weems replied and turned to Blumfeld. 'You left orders not to be disturbed, sir, and I have already attended to the matter of a replacement for Rosenthal.'

'Why'd you figure Rosenthal wouldn't be back?' Brad inquired.

'A most unstable young man, sir. I fear steady employment was not for him.'

'Thanks for your time, sir,' Brad said, turning to Blumfeld. 'I'm sorry about what happened here. Would it be possible for somebody to drive Miss Fayde's car to the Chadwick Building? She's in no condition to drive. I'll pay the return cab fare.'

'The gardener, Montez, could attend to it, sir,' Weems suggested.

'See to it,' grunted Blumfeld. 'And you, Counter, keep that partner of your's away from here. I don't want my wife involved in any more—judo lessons.'

'She won't be back,' Brad promised grimly and walked from the room. He left the house and went to where a dejected Alice sat in his M.G. Looking down at her, he saw something was missing. 'Where's your bag?'

'At home,' she answered, just a touch defiantly.

Swinging into his car without another word, Brad drove down the path and from the Blumfeld place. He gave savage concentration to handling the M.G. and did not as much as look at the girl. At last Alice broke the silence.

'She lied about it, Brad.'

'And you're still a deputy, not facing an assault rap or the Disciplinary Board,' Brad answered, his voice brittle and angry. 'And neither am I.'

'But I owe *that* to her!' Alice spat out.

'You ought to have thought of that before you went to see her. But you went looking for a fight and got one. If you'd been handling the matter officially, you'd have called me and brought your bag along.'

With female lack of logic, Alice turned on Brad. 'Stop this car ri——'

'So help me, Alice,' Brad growled. 'If you start to go woman on me, I'll slap your teeth in. Now sit there and don't speak until you can talk sense.'

Alice relapsed into silence, tears trickling down her cheeks. Nor did Brad offer to speak to her until the spasm ended. At last Alice regained partial control of herself and, looking around, discovered they were still in Upton Heights.

'I'm taking you to see a doctor,' Brad told her. 'You need fixing up a mite.'

Although Alice had heard of the doctor Brad took her to see, she never expected to find herself as his patient for he ran the most exclusive practice in the city. However, the doctor greeted Brad as a hunting and fishing friend and told Alice to go into his office.

With her wounds treated, Alice rode in Brad's car to her apartment where she changed back into her working clothes. When she tried to express her thanks, he laughed them off, saying that if one hoped to succeed in any field one must take good care of one's senior partner.

Shortly before four o'clock Alice and Brad entered the sheriff's office squadroom and found both watches present. The other deputies looked her over with interest, word of the attack on her having spread around. Coming over, Grantley studied Alice's two blackened eyes, swollen lip and a couple of plaster-covered places on her cheeks where nails had left their marks.

'How about coming over to my place tonight, Alice?' he asked, grinning. 'I'd like to show Vera that she's a heap better off as a retired policewoman.'

All the others had some remark to make, the usual razzing a well-liked member of their department received when sporting battle-scars.

'What the hell happened to you?' asked Joan when she finally managed to get Alice alone, for she knew her friend had only one shiner when she left the apartment to come on watch that morning,

'Let it drop, Joan,' Alice pleaded.

'Sure, honey, the boys were rough enough on you. Only they don't often get to see a woman officer mussed up. Say, a fuzz from Greevers called, said he'd followed your man to the Acme Bonding Company on Lennon. Then D.M.V. came through and said the car you wanted made belongs to Thomas Yardley. I ran a check on him, he's a punk who acts as go-between for Caldicott.'

'Thanks,' Alice answered. 'I'm going in to see Jack.'

'Bucking for sick leave?' smiled Joan.

'I may not have to,' Alice replied soberly and walked slowly from the room.

Rising, Joan went to where Brad sat at his team's desk. 'What's with our gal, Brad?' she asked. 'Who handed her the other shiner?'

'Not me, that's for sure,' he replied.

McCall entered the office and came straight to Brad's desk, a large envelope in his hand.

'I.C.R. just flew this in,' he said, and for once his voice showed some trace of excitement. 'The F.B.I. made those fingerprints we sent in. On their civilian files, which's what took them so long. George Henry Sleath, a section eighter discharged from the army on psychopathic grounds. Released from hospital as cured six years ago. Present whereabouts unknown.'

Taking the official mug-shot and record card from McCall, Brad studied the front view and both profiles of a thin-faced man. Then he lifted the composite drawing of 'Sloane' from the desk. Though not exactly alike, they showed enough resemblance for him to feel certain that the man the witnesses tried to describe and Sleath were one and the same.

'There's a lab report on your desk,' Joan remarked, taking the card from Brad's hands.

Brad picked up the report and read it. Comparison tests established that one of the hair oil samples from the pillow at the Junior Street garage matched up with that on Sloane's pillow in the Bestwick Hotel room.

'Which makes Sleath our man for the Junior Street torch job,' McCall remarked. 'Wonder why.'

'The car was there, maybe the owner saw Sleath and his partner and they rubbed him because they were afraid he'd start running scared,' Brad guessed.

'Looks that way,' agreed the watch commander. 'You and Alice had best start hitting the hotels, see if you can pick up either Sleath or Jackson.'

'I'll tend to it as soon as she comes back,' Brad promised.

Only he knew that what he meant was *if* she came back in. Knowing why she asked for an interview with the sheriff, Brad could only hope that Jack Tragg took a lenient view of Alice's actions that morning and did not suspend the girl from duty prior to taking her before the County Commissioners' Disciplinary Board and having her broken to policewoman if not discharged from the Department completely.

CHAPTER SIXTEEN

ALMOST half an hour passed before Alice returned to the office. The day watch had logged off and Brad was alone when she entered, walking in the stiff-back, rigid-faced manner of a woman fighting to hold down tears. Still holding herself tightly in check, she studied the F.B.I.'s mug shots of Sleath and glanced at S.I.B. report.

'Mac says for us to hit the hotels and see if we can trace Sleath,' Brad told her.

'L-let's do it then,' she replied.

Not until riding shotgun in SO 12 did Alice break down. For almost three minutes she sobbed bitterly. At last the fit passed and she turned a wet, red-eyed face to her partner.

'I—I t-told Jack. Lord, I've never seen him so angry. He said I'd not only loused up any chance we might have had of nailing Marla, but that I queered the best opportunity we're likely to get to nail Caldicott's hide to the wall. And I did it too.'

'Yep, you did it too,' agreed Brad.

'I thought he'd suspend me, or break me,' Alice went on, ignoring the interruption. 'But instead he just bawled me out.'

'And you deserved it.'

'Don't you start, Brad Counter!' Alice wailed. 'I know I deserved it. I deserve breaking and being put back pounding a traffic beat. Only y-you d-don't even think I'm fit for that.'

'Knock it off, Alice!' Brad snapped. 'You're acting like a green rookie getting her wrist slapped for the first time.'

'I've been bawled out before,' Alice admitted. 'But by B.W.O. sergeants. Why Jack Tragg didn't even treat me as a woman. He said——'

'He treated you the way he'd treat any deputy who made a damned fool mistake and nearly wound up before the Disciplinary Board.'

Alice stared at Brad, her mouth hanging open. Suddenly she saw the bawling-out in its true perspective. Ever since entering the sheriff's office she had been striving for equal acceptance with the men. Now it seemed that Jack Tragg had accepted her. That was why he did not treat her as a woman, even a policewoman, but handled her as he would a member—a *useful* member—of his staff who had made a damned fool mistake, but who could be relied upon not to repeat her folly.

'We—we'll try the hotels like the Newnes and Bestwick first,' she said and her old voice had returned. 'Might be best to hit the temperance places first.'

'Yes sir, ma'am,' grinned Brad, throwing her a salute. 'You're the boss—again.'

'After what happened today?'

'What did happen today?' Brad countered. 'Hey though, before we get back to normal I'd like to give you a last order.'

'Feel free,' she smiled.

'Then you dry off your face and put some make-up on. Happen I'm seen out with you like you look now, word might get around that I beat my girls into submission. That would plumb ruin the family name.'

Looking into the car's rear-view mirror, Alice studied the state of her face and gave a little squeal of embarrassment at what she saw. Hurriedly she dug into her bag and produced the necessary items to repair the damage. With feminine vanity satisfied, she settled down to the business of making a partial search of the city's hotels in the hope of flushing out Tom Cord's killers.

One team of deputies, even in a fast modern car, could not hope to visit every hotel and rooming-house in the city, at least not in a single day. However, most crooks could be relied on to follow a set pattern; using the same methods of operation in the commission of the crime, inhabiting the same type of accommodation in between jobs. The professional killers had stayed in middle-rent type hotels, Sleath using one which prohibited the sale of liquor within its walls. Other temperance hotels would be the first objectives in Alice and Brad's search.

Even knowing the city as well as she did, Alice could not remember the name of every middle-rent place; and Brad, a comparative newcomer, knew only a few, none of them of temperance persuasion. However, Rockabye County maintained a highly efficient department to supply the law-enforcement officers with such information.

Taking up the car's microphone, Alice called Central Control and requested that Records and Identification be asked to send a list of middle-rent hotels and rooming-houses. Normally she would have telephoned for the details, but time did not allow her to follow normal channels.

'Jack told me he couldn't hold the stake-outs much longer,' she explained. 'So we'd best hurry and come up with some lead, Brad, or he'll have to cancel the close-off and put the men back on normal duty.'

'Sure, Alice. Let's hope we get a lead.'

'Know something, Brad? I think they're still in the city.'

After studying Sleath's record card—from the F.B.I. files, Speedphotoed to I.C.R. in Austin and flown to Gusher City—Alice felt even more certain that Brad called the play right when he claimed that professional killers shot her uncle. Such men worked from an efficient criminal organisation which covered every aspect and detail when sending men out on a contract.

Having reached her decision, a thought began to nag at Alice. With such an organisation behind them, why had Sleath and 'Jackson' committed the blunder of booking seats on a flight out of the city? The killers would know how quickly the law moved when a peace officer was killed, yet they made for the airport; one of the first places to be covered by the law. Of course Alice knew that sooner or later every criminal made a slip, but she felt curious as to why two obviously experienced men would make such an elementary mistake.

For almost three hours they combed the city, following the list sent out by R. and I., visiting hotels and rooming-houses and showing the composite drawing and mug shots of the wanted men, but without results. A shooting was reported in

Evans Hill, but on calling in to Central Control Alice learned that Rafferty and Chu had gone to handle the investigation.

'And that's the last of the list,' Brad remarked as they left a rooming-house soon after the shooting call. 'What now, the flea-belt?'

'I'd go for the more expensive places,' Alice answered. 'We could——'

'Cen-Con to Unit SO 12,' interrupted the dispatcher's voice.

Taking up the microphone, Alice replied, 'Unit SO 12 by.'

'Go "Code Three" to 79A Dannert Street, Evans Hill Division. "Code One"?'

'Roger, over and out.'

Even before Alice finished speaking, Brad reached out a hand to switch on the car's red light, then he jabbed the siren button and the Oldsmobile picked up speed, following the dispatcher's orders to treat the call as an emergency.

Racing across town, with siren screaming and red light flashing its warning, Brad slid through the traffic towards the address given by the dispatcher. Situated on the fringe of Evans Hill, 79A Dannert Street proved to be an apartment house of the cheaper type. The usual crowd stood around outside and several official vehicles parked along the street before the building.

Alice and Brad left the Oldsmobile with the other cars, identified themselves to the patrolman on the door and entered the building. A small knot of people who lived in the house, a couple of reporters and a pair of patrolmen stood around in the hall, but the deputies ignored them. Going up to the first floor, Alice and Brad went along the passage and were admitted to the death room.

Nothing had been moved and a photographer worked at recording the scene of the crime. The victim lay just inside the door; a medium-sized, stocky man in his early thirties, wearing a pair of dark blue slacks and a white shirt. There were three holes in the front of the shirt; large holes from which the blood had now ceased to pump.

'Alice, Brad,' Rafferty greeted, coming forward. 'Thought you'd want to be in on this.'

'Why, Mick?' Alice asked.

'It sounds like the two you want did the killing.'

Alice and Brad exchanged glances, then turned their attention back to Rafferty. However, from the bulky deputy, Brad dropped his gaze to the holes in the shirt. Even with the clotting of blood, the size of the holes was plainly apparent. Brad knew plenty about firearms, including enough of the damage a bullet inflicted to know that no small or medium calibre weapon—from .22 up to .38 Special—inflicted the wounds. No sir, the big, angry holes came as a result of the passage of a large calibre bullet. *Three* large calibre bullets, any one of which would have been fatal.

'Sure wanted him dead,' Brad remarked.

'That's what they're paid for,' Alice pointed out.

'Sure,' agreed Brad. 'Only three .45 bullets are a tolerable heap of lead to sink into a man, especially when one would kill him.'

'Can I start work?' Tom Chu asked from the bed, directing his question to the photographer.

'Feel free,' answered the technician. 'I'm done here.'

Taking up the coat which lay on a chair, Tom started to empty its pockets and list the contents. On removing the wallet, he called Brad over to double check on it. Alice stood at the door with Rafferty and her eyes went around the room. It was a normally furnished place for its type. A belted trench-coat and fedora hat hung on the outside pegs of the wardrobe and a brown suitcase rested on top.

'How'd you know who killed him?' she asked.

'An old guy along the hall was coming out of his room when he saw two jaspers at this door. One of them, the taller, slimmer, had a revolver with a silencer on its barrel. Fanned three shots into the victim. Then the other, he fits 'Jackson's' description, closed the door and they walked away! The old guy ducked back before they saw him, which's lucky for him, then waited until he was well sure that they'd gone and came down to call us in. We've put a general call out for them and we thought we'd best get you over here.'

'I'm pleased you did,' Alice told him. 'Who's the victim?'

'*Registered* under the name of Thomas Flowers, came in yesterday morning.'

'Is he Thomas Flowers?' asked Alice, noticing the emphasis Rafferty placed on the first word.

'Not unless my eyes are going back on me. I make him Tommy Farson, a high-power we put away for seven on an 1163. Thought he was safe in the Walls for another two years at least. I called the office and asked them to check on whether the governor of the Walls knows old Tommy's out.'

'We'd've heard if he'd broke out,' Alice objected.

A knock at the door interrupted any further discussion and a patrolman looked into the room. 'Cen-Con just called,' he said. 'They checked Farson, he was released from the Clemmens Unit on Sunday at noon and given a railroad ticket to Gusher City.'

Brad shot across the room, halting before the startled patrolman after almost knocking Rafferty and Alice over. 'Say that again!' he snapped.

'Have you flipped, Brad?' Rafferty growled.

'Which unit did you say?' Brad repeated to the patrolman, ignoring Rafferty's question.

'The Clemmens Unit,' answered the patrolman. 'He was paroled out——'

The words fell on deaf ears for Brad had already swung towards Alice. One look at her face told Brad she followed his line of thought. The Clemmens Unit was a prison farm based at Brazoria.

'It's coincidence,' Alice breathed, in a tone which meant 'it must be coincidence, it can't be anything else'.

Turning, Brad crossed the room and pointed to the hat and coat, then at the suitcase. 'Look at them, Alice. Tom was wearing a belted trenchcoat and a hat like that——'

'And carrying a suitcase!' Alice breathed. 'If Farson left Brazoria on the West-bound, he'd reach Gusher City at nine-fifty.'

'Only he didn't come out of the depot,' Brad finished. 'Tom walked out.'

'And the killers cut down the wrong man,' Rafferty growled. 'There's no wonder we couldn't find anybody with a motive.'

'It explains everything,' Alice said. 'Why the killers chanced booking a flight out. They never expected us to move so quickly when it was an ex-con they hit, or thought they hit. But why didn't Farson come off the train?'

'He's pretty flush with money,' Brad answered. 'And there's

a bus ticket in his wallet, it's from Langtry. He must have dropped off there to pick up some cash before coming to town.'

Rafferty scratched his head. 'Which don't explain to me how the killers knew what train to wait for or how Farson was dressed.'

'Somebody from Gusher City drove down to Brazoria, watched Farson come out and telephoned a description,' Brad explained. 'Only the description fitted two men and the wrong one walked out of the depot.'

'Does that somebody have a name?' Chu asked.

'Yeah, Tommy,' Brad replied, an alum-bitter smile playing on his lips. 'He has a name. I know—— Hell fire! I clean forgot to——'

Without another word Brad turned and dashed from the room. Bounding down the stairs three at a time, he regained control of himself just before he came into sight of the hall. A place like 79A Dannert Street did not offer the luxury of a telephone in every apartment, instead a communal instrument hung on the wall by the door. Brad did not want to make his call in public, but guessed that the building's superintendent had a private telephone in his room.

'Who's the super?' he asked and a short, bald man stepped forward. 'I'd like to use your telephone, sir.'

'There's one——' the super began.

'A private phone,' Brad cut in.

Something in the big deputy's voice warned the man not to make difficulties. Turning, the super led Brad to his apartment, opened the door and allowed the deputy to enter.

Taking up the telephone, Brad dialled D.M.V.'s number at Headquarters and said, 'Deputy Counter. Make the licence of a '58 Dodge hardtop owned by Ben Rosenthal for me. He was working at the Blumfeld place on Beaunavista Avenue. R. and I. will have his home address. When you get the number, have it put out as a general and notify surrounding counties. Sure, I want him picked up. Can do it? Thanks.'

Hanging up the telephone, Brad cursed himself for not having made the call much earlier. Rosenthal's flight proved his guilt in the matter of the abortive attempt to ambush Brad, but the deputy wanted the Blumfeld's chauffeur for another reason. Unless Brad was sadly mistaken, Rosenthal's description of the newly-released Tommy Farson brought about Tom Cord's death.

'Did you know Farson?' Brad asked the super.

'Who?' yelped the man.

'Flowers.'

'Naw! He come here 'cause we had an "Apartment Vacant" sign out. Paid the nut in advance, which's all I ask.'

'Did he have any visitors?'

'None that I know about.'

'Make any calls?'

A shifty glint came into the super's eyes and he dropped his voice even though he had closed the door on entering the apartment. 'Wouldn't want it to get no further. Folks might think I snooped on 'em. Only this ain't the best built place in town and——'

'Get to it,' Brad growled.

'Well, I just happened to hear him talking on the phone to some doll.'

'Did he mention her name?'

'Naw.'

'Then how——?' asked Brad.

'Easy enough. He said something like "You come on down here, honey-baby, and we'll talk things out." Now does that sound like he was talking to a man?'

'Reckon not. When was this?'

'Early this afternoon, maybe around three time,' the super answered. 'Say, there ain't anything in this, is there? I mean like newspaper stories?'

'There may be, only don't try to peddle them your life story.'

'Smart-alec cop!' sniffed the super as Brad turned and walked out of the room. 'Never even paid me for the use of the phone.'

Up in the death room Alice, Rafferty and Chu stared after the departing Brad. At last Rafferty gave a sigh.

'He was never like that until he started working with a woman.'

'Just for that, Mick Rafferty,' Alice answered, 'I won't marry you ever.'

It had become a standing joke for Rafferty to ask Alice to marry him at least once a day, disregarding the fact that he already possessed a wife and three children to whom he was devoted.

'Then there is hope for humble Oriental fuzz,' grinned Tommy Chu, sounding and looking like a 'B' movie Chinese detective.

'What's this all about, Alice?' asked Rafferty, becoming serious once more.

'It's the break we wanted,' she replied. 'I can't go too far yet, Mick, but I know why Uncle Tom was killed. I don't know why she wanted Farson dead though.'

'She?' prompted Rafferty.

'Let's give this room a good turn over,' Alice suggested, ignoring the question. 'We might be wasting our time, but it's worth a try.'

Alice went to where the suitcase now lay open upon the bed. It was empty, but that did not stop her bending down and examining the bottom lining.

'Something?' asked Rafferty, seeing her tense slightly as she ducked her head down into the case.

'I think so. Loan me a knife one of you guys.'

Taking a switch-blade knife from his pocket, Chu flicked out the blade and passed it hilt-first to Alice. Working carefully, she started to cut through the lining at the bottom of the case. It took time and Brad returned before she finished opening up a false bottom to the case. Under the flap of leather she found a large envelope and took it out.

'What's that?' Brad asked as she tipped out the envelope's contents.

'A marriage certificate and photograph,' Alice replied, turning the items over. 'Thomas James Farson and Martha Lar——'

Her voice died away as if she had been struck dumb. Even though she suspected what she would find, on seeing the certificate, it still came as a shock to have her suspicions proved correct. Taking the certificate from Alice's limp and unresisting fingers, Brad turned them so he could take a closer look. The certificate covered the picture, obscuring the details on its surface.

'Thomas Farson and Martha Larraine Bixby,' he read, wondering why the names should affect Alice as they did.

Taking the certificate away. Brad looked down at the photograph and a low exclamation left his lips. It was a glossy print of the dead man when younger and clearly enjoying life. He stood facing the camera, a broad grin on his face and a beautiful girl on his arm.

Although the girl had shoulder long hair done in a peek-a-boo style over the left eye, and stood laughing as she pointed to a thin ring on her left hand's third finger, Brad recognised her. Only now the hair was much shorter—and she wore another man's wedding ring.

'Let's go pick her up, Brad,' Alice said flatly.

'You?' he asked.

'I can do it—now.'

Before they reached the door, the patrolman who brought the last message appeared again.

'Deputy McCall's on the phone. He wants to speak to Fayde and Counter.'

'Now what?' Alice asked.

'Best way to find out'd be go and see,' Brad replied.

On reaching the superintendent's room, Alice took up the receiver and heard McCall's Scottish burr over the wires. 'Alice, tell Brad his Uncle Pete just called in and wants him to get over to the Tex-Mex Importing Company warehouse on Beale Street. Says there's a couple of rats inside.'

'Tell Mac we're on our way and ask him to stand by with help,' Brad said when Alice passed on the message.

He had no Uncle Pete, but Izzy Bergen always used that name when calling the office to contact Tom Cord and pass on information.

CHAPTER SEVENTEEN

DESPITE the urgent nature of their business, Brad did not use the siren or red light while driving the short distance from Dannert Street to the Beale Street business section. Bergen's message implied that two badly wanted men were in the warehouse and they might be scared off if they heard a police car's siren.

'I wonder who they are,' Alice said as Brad cut the speeding Oldsmobile through the traffic.

'Maybe Bergen's just trying me out,' Brad replied. 'They could be anybody.'

Alice nodded her agreement. An informer learning something he could sell looked for the most profitable market. If Bergen learned anything that came under the sheriff's office jurisdiction, he would, with Tom Cord dead, contact Brad. Like all Tom's informers, Bergen probably wondered what kind of remuneration he could expect from his new employer and took the first opportunity to find out.

Slowing down the car as he entered Beale Street, Brad saw Bergen step momentarily into the light of a street lamp, then fade off into the shadows again. Brad waited until his car passed through the light before stopping. Climbing out, he walked around and leaned on the right side of the car, waiting for Bergen to come to him.

'Got a hot one, Mr Counter,' the informer said. 'Two pistols fresh from a hit.'

Nothing Bergen could have said would arouse Brad's interest as much as that short speech. There had only been one hit, killing, in Gusher City that day and Brad was very interested in finding the men who did it. However, he knew better than let his interest and eagerness show.

'I need more than that,' he commented.

In the car, Alice listened and smiled. Having seen her uncle handle an informer she recognised the technique. Brad appeared to have learned his lessons well.

'Sure,' Bergen answered. 'I got word that there was a contract out on Tommy Farson, only thought it was a bum steer, him being in stir. Then damn me if I don't hear he's out and around town. So I go over there and stake out his pad. Saw the two pistols arrive. They're from the East, I've heard of them although they've never worked this part of Texas before. Saw them go in and come out and tailed them. They split up, I went after the thin guy. He led me here and as far as I know they're still inside.'

Which left a whole lot unexplained, although Brad knew better than go into the matter further. Bergen sold information to more than the police, as Brad knew, and had contacts in every major city of Texas. Just how much he knew about the killing would never come out. Possibly the man behind the killers made use of Bergen's specialised talents to locate Farson. Then the informer decided to increase his take by fingering the two killers to the law. Maybe the organisation had decided that Sleath and 'Jackson' were slipping and used Bergen to have the killers removed in a manner which would not arouse suspicion among others of their class in the mob.

Whatever the reason, no matter how Bergen came by his knowledge, Brad did not care. All that mattered was Bergen's information leading Brad to the men who killed his partner.

'Anything on Tom?' Brad asked, watching Bergen's face.

'If anybody knows anything, they're not talking.'

Nothing in the informer's voice or attitude hinted that he lied. Brad felt willing to bet that Bergen had not connected the two killings.

'Can we get inside?' Alice asked.

'Side door's still open, I saw to that,' answered Bergen. 'Did I do all right by you, Mr Counter?'

'I'll tell you better when we come out,' Brad answered and slipped two ten dollar bills into the man's hand. 'See you, Izzy.'

'You know where to find me,' Bergen replied and faded off into the darkness.

Brad guessed he had gauged the right amount for the

information. Of course, if Alice and he picked up the two men, and they proved to be worthwhile, Bergen would expect and receive a bonus for his services.

After Bergen left, Alice took up the car's microphone, changed frequencies and called Central Control. Her call was relayed directly to McCall's office and Alice quickly explained the situation to the watch commander.

'Tell him I'm going in,' Brad growled.

'*We're* going in, Mac,' Alice corrected.

'Give me five minutes if you can,' McCall answered. 'I'll move in what cars I can from around you.'

'Tell them no "Code Three",' Alice requested. 'We want to bottle them in the warehouse, not take after them on the streets.'

'I *had* thought of that,' McCall replied dryly.

'Sorry, Mac, I always talk too much when I'm scared.'

A low chuckle reached Alice's ears. 'My wife doesna need to be scared, lass. Five minutes if you can.'

'Yo! Have the cars cover the entrances, but tell the crews not to come busting in if they hear shooting.'

'I'll tend to it and come down myself. Good luck. Over and out.'

The call had been overheard by the dispatcher and already she sent out messages which started four cars moving towards the warehouse, speeding in silence as Alice requested.

Leaving the car, Alice and Brad walked along a side street and halted by the warehouse's glass-panelled door. While Alice checked on the time, Brad looked through the panel into the building. At that moment Brad blessed the Fire Department regulations which insisted that all such buildings be kept illuminated internally as an aid in case of fire. Although not well lit, the lights gave him a clear view of the inside of the building. Rows of stacked boxes covered the floor, split by lanes along which fork-lift trucks could manoeuvre. The door at which Brad stood lay about three-quarters of the way along the building and from where he stood, he could see a flight of iron stairs leading up to what appeared to be a checker's office that overlooked the entire warehouse. A stronger light than the rest glowed in the office and a shape passed before its opaque window.

'Let's go,' Alice breathed, checking that the five minutes had elapsed.

Gently Brad turned the door handle with his left hand; his right drew the big Colt as soon as she spoke. Easing the door open, he stepped inside and Alice, Cobra in hand, followed on his heels. Their plan of campaign was to move through the lanes of boxes and take cover where they could watch the stairs. Then when the two killers came down, get the drop on them with as little chance of retaliation as possible.

Only things went wrong.

Even as the deputies entered, the checking office's door opened. Alice had closed the door and was just turning when she heard Brad's low hiss and raised her eyes to the stairs.

Alice and Brad studied the two men who emerged from the office, comparing what they saw with the composite drawing produced by the police artist. The man they knew as 'Jackson' led the way, a suitcase in his hand, his topcoat over a suit and a fedora hat on his head; the artist had not done a bad job from the witnesses' impression of 'Jackson'. However, Sleath drew most of the deputies' attention. A peaked uniform cap sat on his head and he wore a poorly-fitting cadet-grey chauffeur's uniform, the tunic open.

Darting cautious glances around, Sleath started to follow 'Jackson' down the stairs. Brad and Alice, fifty yards away, tried to get out of sight, but their movement caught the slim killer's eye. Swinging around, Sleath sent his right hand stabbing under the tunic and fetched out the Smith & Wesson. The gun no longer bore its silencer and bellowed loud in the confines of the warehouse. Taken from a pointed fire position, the bullet passed between the two deputies.

Instantly Brad moved, left hand thrusting Alice to safety behind the nearest row of boxes, right raising his automatic. Only Brad knew better than rely on a one-handed pointed fire aim at a distance of fifty yards. From shoving Alice to safety, the left hand carried on up, joining the right as it extended shoulder high. Using the double-handed technique devised by Sheriff Jack Weaver of Lancaster, California, Brad prepared to shoot. The Weaver stance had been perfected for just such a situation that Brad now faced and a trained man could take it fast.

Legs apart, body erect, arms extended, left hand supporting the right wrist, Brad took sight along the Colt's barrel and touched off a shot. Fifty yards away, Sleath rocked under the impact of the bullet and a second, following on the speeding heels of the first, ripped into him. The powerful bullets flung Sleath backwards, his body striking the stairs' guard rail and falling over, the gun dropping from his hand.

Dropping the suitcase he carried, 'Jackson' sprang down the stairs. Twice the big automatic crashed and each time the gunman felt the wind of the passing shots. Only luck and the speed with which he moved saved 'Jackson' during the short time he stayed in Brad's sight. Then he passed from view behind the boxes, reached the foot of the stairs and hurled himself across the open space to the nearest cover. Halting by a stack of boxes on the edge of the wide central lane, 'Jackson' looked around him. Escape had been cut off from one door, but each side possessed a way out.

Even as 'Jackson' turned his eyes to the west entrance, he heard the hideous banshee wail of a police siren from outside. Before he could tear his eyes to the north wall, a similar sound rose there, and at south and east. Hearing the shots, the waiting cars gave notice of their presence, warning the criminal that he was surrounded. 'Jackson' glanced at the stairs and shook his head. A warped sense of chivalry prevented him from making use of the avenue of escape offered him in the office, even if he made it to the top of the stairs alive.

Almost before 'Jackson' went out of sight, Brad sprang into action. The big deputy bounded down the nearest lane, forgetting that he did not have the backing of Tom Cord. However, Alice showed her grasp of the situation. Swiftly she ran along the line of boxes and on reaching the last one peered around. No sign of 'Jackson', but she prepared to handle his appearance by taking up the barricade stance. Placing her left hand flat against the edge of the box, she allowed her thumb to extend beyond it. Swiftly she rested her right wrist in the shallow V the thumb and box formed. By moving her left foot until it almost touched the wall, and swinging her right leg back, Alice twisted her torso behind the cover, yet stood easily while exposing only the Cobra-filled right hand, left thumb and small portion of the right side of her head. While Alice had never fired her gun at a human being, she knew just what to do and was prepared to do it.

Sprinting down the narrow lane, eyes alert for the first sign of danger, Brad felt a cold satisfaction. Ever since killing the young man outside the Beverly Arms, doubts had nagged at Brad. Could he have taken time for a more careful aim and wounded the punk instead of killing? Ought he to have challenged, given the other a chance to surrender? Although he knew the answer to both questions was 'no', the doubts remained. Going up against 'Jackson', a professional killer not a gun-crazy doped-up punk, ought to satisfy Brad's misgivings.

Brad reached the central lane, stopping and peering around the corner. First he saw Sleath lying sprawled on the ground by the side of the stairs and knew he could discount the slim killer as a factor. Then Brad caught a glimpse of 'Jackson' as the man moved out to cross the lane at the stairs end.

Flame spurted from the gun 'Jackson' held, its lead kicking splinters from the box by Brad's head. Following his training, Brad pumped two shots in return, driving 'Jackson' back into cover. In that brief moment Brad had seen 'Jackson's' weapon and knew it to be an automatic similar in shape to his own, but, from its sound, of lighter calibre. Which meant the killer held either a Smith & Wesson 9-mm, a Colt Commander, a Browning P-35 or one of the other medium calibre models based on John Moses Browning's design; most of which carried eight or nine bullets in the magazine, although the P-35 held thirteen. No matter which model automatic the man held, it gave him several more bullets than remained in Brad's Government Model Colt.

With that in mind, Brad prepared to rectify the situation.

'All right, Jackson!' he shouted. 'We've got you bottled in. Throw out the gun and come out with your hands raised.'

'Come and get me!' Jordan answered, the name 'Jackson' showing him where he made his first mistake.

'We'll do that too,' Brad called back. 'I'm asking for the last time. Come out with empty hands.'

'Go to hell!'

Brad had never expected the man to surrender. With the

electric chair waiting, unless his own organisation silenced him before he could squeal on them, Jordan would not give up as long as a single chance of escape remained. However, the pause for conversation gave Brad his chance to make an adjustment in his armament.

Even as he called the first words, Brad took one of his spare magazines from the concealed pouch in his jacket. His right thumb pressed the automatic's release stud and its magazine slid out into his waiting left hand. The instant the partially empty magazine slid clear, Brad thrust home the loaded reserve which had been gripped between thumb and forefinger of his left hand. Only a second elapsed, but at the end of that time Brad held a gun with eight bullets in it ready for use.

Suddenly Brad thrust himself into the open, darting across the lane towards the next higher gap at the far side, getting closer to where Jordan hid. Jordan's pistol spat twice, the bullets missing Brad by inches and the big deputy fired once as he ran. Always a good scorer on the Mexican Defence Course —a test in which the shooter aimed at a line of six targets while running towards or parallel to them—Brad sent his lead close enough to prevent the killer taking a careful aim and so reached his next cover safety. However, Brad found that he still could not obtain a clear aim at Jordan.

Halting in his new position, Brad prepared to make another rush. While knowing how well Alice could handle a gun, he did not wish to leave her to face the killer; and at any moment Jordan might try to get by the girl as being safer than tangling with a man.

At the end of the lane, Jordan reached the same conclusion. Chivalry was all right in its place, but that place ended when one's neck was at stake. He moved to the next box, hiding in a gap left by removing one stack, and cautiously advanced. Then he saw the little of Alice showing from her barricade stance position. His automatic cracked and the Cobra spat back, its bullet coming close enough to warn Jordan that the girl could handle her gun with some skill.

Swinging around, Jordan gave his thoughts to the main danger. With the big male deputy out of the way, he might be able to sneak around, grab the woman and use her as a hostage. The other cops would not burst in while the shooting went on, for they would be more hindrance than help to the two already inside.

Without his thinking about it, Jordan had counted Brad's shots. Two cutting Sleath down, two more as he himself bounded for safety, a further pair on their first sight of each other along the lane, one more during his dash across the lane. Seven in all. The deputy used a Colt Government Model automatic, seven rounds in the magazine and one in the chamber. Which meant he had only one bullet left in his gun. Jordan figured the edge lay on his side.

Once more Brad burst into sight and Jordan exposed a little of himself to draw a shot, pumping a couple of bullets along the lane. The big automatic roared an answer to the challenge.

'Eight!' thought Jordan and sprang into the centre of the lane.

Two things saved Brad at that moment: first, Jordan felt so sure he had the deputy at his mercy that he took his time; second, Brad's superb speed of reaction. While Brad did not expect the man to appear, he could guess why Jordan took such a chance. However, Brad gave no thought to that. Skidding to a halt, he went into his combat crouch, the Colt lining and locking. Four times Brad squeezed the trigger, his bullets ripping into the chest of Tom Cord's killer. The fourth bullet struck home before the first empty, ejected case landed on the floor.

Jordan went hurling backwards, his Browning clattering to the floor. Any one of the bullets would have been fatal, for they patterned in a three inch group on the left side of his body. He crashed to the floor at the foot of the stairs, his back a hideous mess of shattered, splintered bone, torn flesh and oozing blood.

Moving forward, gun ready for use, Brad approached the dead killer. Suddenly lead ripped by his head and he heard the flat slap of a bullet breaking the air by his ear. From above him came the crack of a light calibre pistol. Instantly Brad looked upwards, starting to bring his Colt to the Weaver Stance, but he did not open fire on his attacker.

She stood at the head of the stairs; a mink coat covered an expensive travelling suit, a dainty hat perched on her immaculately coiffured blonde hair, make-up hid most of the fight damage on her face. In her left hand she held a pair of sunglasses—the right gripped the butt of a Colt Woodsman .22 automatic in a manner which showed she had an idea how to use it.

Again the gun spat and Brad felt a .22 Long Rifle bullet stir his hair in passing. Yet even to save his life he could not open fire on a woman.

'Marla!'

The word, almost screamed, brought the blonde's eyes and gun swinging in the speaker's direction. Alice sprang from cover as she shouted, going into the Weaver Stance but not shooting. Savagely Marla pressed her gun's trigger. Three times she fired down at Alice without a shot coming in return. The fourth bullet struck just ahead of Alice, ricocheting up between her spread-apart legs and ripping her skirt without touching flesh. All the shots had come close to Alice, but th last warned her she must do something. Taking aim touched off two shots, riding the wicked kick of t weight Cobra and sighting the second bullet before it.

Marla jerked as lead struck her, tried to re-align her gun, failed and let it sag towards the floor. Then her legs buckled, she staggered, went over the top step and pitched down the entire flight. Landing on the floor, she lay sprawled out, her blonde hair mingling with Jordan's spreading blood.

'Alice!' Brad said, swinging towards her. 'Are you all right?'

'Sh-she never touched me,' Alice replied, her legs feeling suddenly weak. 'Get the men in, Brad. I——'

At which point Alice slipped to the floor in a faint.

CHAPTER EIGHTEEN

MARLA BLUMFELD lived for two days, with doctors fighting to save her. On the second morning, she recovered enough to speak and asked for Alice to be brought to see her. It seemed that Marla wanted to try to straighten out her tangled life and Alice found a pallid, haggard Blumfeld at the hospital when she arrived; Weems, as imperturbable as ever by his master's side.

Lying on the bed, her face drawn and pale, Marla looked from Alice to the police stenographer who sat in the corner of the room.

'Hello, Alice,' she greeted weakly. 'It's strange how life goes. That it should be you who——'

'I'd like to say I'm sorry, Marla,' Alice replied. 'But it was through you that Uncle Tom died.'

'I know,' Marla admitted. 'Lord. What a stinking mess I made of my life. Marla Bixby, the girl who was going to be somebody, who would take Hollywood and shake it until it rattled.'

Slowly the story came out. Despite her mother's hopes, Marla never made the grade in Hollywood. Her screen tests showed that she possessed little talent, and at that time a beautiful body was not a passport to film stardom. All her mother's money went in a vain attempt to establish Marla, or even get her started, then a car crash left the girl alone and broke. Although the film industry had no use for Marla, she found her beautiful body opened the door into another branch of the entertainment business. Not a high-class branch at the level she joined, but one which at least kept her fed. Marla became a stripper on one of the cheaper circuits.

During one of her shows, she met Tommy Farson and married him. Not until after their wedding did she learn that he was a high-power, working with a stick-up mob. At that time Farson's luck ran high and Marla lived well. Although she took no part in his criminal activities, she met many of his underworld contacts; including a man who proved useful in later years. The first rosy flush of the marriage had worn off when Farson's luck ran out and a Texas judge sent him to the Walls for seven years—by a coincidence it had been in Gusher City where the law laid hands on him—and Marla had been pleased to see him out of her life.

Returning to the stripper-circuit, Marla reached Reno with a slightly better-grade show and there she met Blumfeld. They fell in love and the girl accepted his offer of marriage without mentioning that she already possessed a husband. Although at Reno, Marla made no attempt to obtain a divorce from Farson, fearing that Blumfeld would hear of it and throw her aside. Instead she arranged for word to reach Farson that she had died and felt sure that he would never trace her.

After their marriage, Blumfeld gave up gambling and moved into a legitimate business. The fact that her new home would be in Gusher City caused Marla no concern. Farson believed her dead, to the best of her knowledge, and she could face her old friends as a success with some social standing.

All seemed to be going along fine for Marla when she learned that Farson not only knew of her second, illegal, marriage, but was making inquiries as to her whereabouts. Learning that he was due for parole, she guessed that he would be coming looking for her on his release and would bleed her white under the threat of exposure.

Not daring to tell Blumfeld, and fearing that she might lose her current secure position, Marla made plans. She remembered a contact made during her life with Farson—a man who arranged the hiring of professional killers. Without going into details of how, Marla told of the contract put out on Farson. It had been decided to kill him on his arrival in Gusher City. Left until later, he might contact Marla and establish a link on which the investigating officers could act.

Then a snag arose. Marla had destroyed every photograph of Farson and could not supply one for the killers' use. While Farson's arrest had been reported in the local newspapers, she dare not try to obtain a picture from their files as that too might lead the law to her. So she used her charm on Rosenthal and made him her aid. Farson had been transferred to the Clemmens Unit and she sent Rosenthal to Brazoria. There the young man waited outside the prison's main entrance, watched Farson leave and telephoned a description of his appearance which Marla had relayed to the killers.

Nobody would ever know why Farson left the train before reaching Gusher City. He did—and Tom Cord, dressed in the same general manner and of a similiar build, walked out of the Southern Pacific Railroad's depot to meet the waiting killers.

Marla admitted hiring the two hookers to help work Alice over. She also told how Rosenthal called in two friends to help fix Brad Counter, fearing that the deputy's offer of a reward might cause the organisation to send its killers to silence everybody who knew anything about the fouled-up contract. While agreeing that she intended to kill Alice, Marla insisted that her assistants knew nothing of it and believed that Marla merely intended to give a rival a thrashing for some reason. Unfortunately, Marla's story did not incriminate Caldicott in any way.

Curiously, Farson did not connect Tom's death with an attempt on his own life. On his arrival in Gusher City, he called Marla and suggested a meeting. Marla telephoned her contact and demanded that she received value for her money. Learning that the two killers were still in town, she made a deal. If they removed Farson, she offered to help them leave Rockabye County. The escape would be simple, if a trifle risky, with Sleath acting as chauffeur in the Cadillac while Jordan rode in the rear seat, posing as Marla's husband. In that way they hoped to pass through the sheriff's road-blocks and get clear of the danger area.

On her arrival at the rendezvous at her husband's warehouse, Marla intended to carry out her side of the bargain and only carried the gun for self-protection. Alice and Brad's arrival spoiled the plan and, knowing she would be found if the building was searched, Marla decided to try to shoot her way out.

'I never could beat you at anything, Alice,' Marla sighed. 'Did you get Rosenthal yet?'

'He was picked up in Fort Worth this morning and they're

shipping him back to us.'

'He was a nasty punk, but apart from Stan that's all I ever rated.'

'You should have told your husband, Marla.'

'You know me,' the girl sighed. 'Always the bri——'

A sudden spasm of pain ripped through her and she arched her back. Instantly the doctor who had been present through the interview moved forward and waved the peace officers from the room. In the passage, Blumfeld loomed up before Alice, his face working in a torrent of agony and bewilderment.

'Why?' he groaned. 'Why did she do it?'

'Maybe because she loved you very much,' Alice answered, trying to give the man comfort. 'Loved you and didn't want you to get hurt.'

'May I suggest that you sit down again, sir?' said Weems, and Blumfeld obeyed without question.

Three hours later Alice left the hospital. There would be no point in her waiting any longer, Marla Blumfeld was dead.

Alice found Brad waiting for her in the squadroom when she returned to the Department of Justice building. Rising as she entered, he walked to meet her.

'It's all over,' she told him. 'Marla is dead.'

'Maybe it's as well,' Brad replied. 'F.I.L. have matched the Smith & Wesson with the bullets found in Farson and the stiff at the Jenner Street torch job and made Sleath for both kills.'

'I thought they would.'

'One thing puzzles me, though,' Brad said as they left the office to report to the sheriff. 'How did you know it was Mrs Blumfeld even before you looked at the picture? The name on the marriage certificate said Martha Larraine Bixby.'

'Marla hated those names and cut them down to make something more erotic-sounding,' Alice replied. 'And my mother's maiden name was Bixby.'

Brad came to a halt as if he had run into an invisible wall. Twisting to face Alice, he looked down at her.

'You mean——?'

'Marla was my cousin—but Tom Cord was my uncle, her's too. I introduced her to the gang when we were kids and always blamed myself for what happened to Viv.'

A shudder ran through Alice's frame and, more to take her mind off what she had done than for any other reason, Brad asked, 'Did Marla know about the photograph and certificate of marriage?'

'She said not when I asked her. If she had, she'd never have sent the killers after him. Come on, let's make our report.'

In the sheriff's office, Jack Tragg listened to the story of the investigation and at last nodded and said:

'You've done a good job, both of you. Those two professional killers have racked up a fair number of hits about the country and are better dead. It's a pity we couldn't've nailed Caldicott, but we've enough to make life mighty uncomfortable for him and we can't win them all.'

'What now, Jack?' asked Brad.

'You need a regular partner, don't you?'

Brad opened his mouth, but the words did not come. Flickering a glance from Jack to Alice, he wondered how to make his request and if it would be acceptable to either of the other occupants of the room.

'Well I——' Brad began.

'Got one in mind,' said Jack, poker-faced and hiding the smile which fought to come. 'Good officer, though a mite hot-tempered at times. Name of Fayde.'

'You mean Alice here?' asked Brad, seeing his wish answered.

'She's the only Fayde we have,' Jack agreed and became serious. 'Look, there are some aspects of our work that can best be handled by a woman and I want a female deputy working full-time on a team on each watch. Reckon you pair can put up with each other?'

'How about it, boss-lady?' Brad inquired. 'Reckon we can?'

Alice smiled back. If she was to work on a team, she could not think of any male partner she would rather have.

'I reckon we can at that,' she replied.

Read more of the team of Alice Fayde and Bradford Counter in

THE $\frac{1}{4}$ SECOND DRAW

The next Rockabye County Novel

A SELECTION OF FINE READING AVAILABLE IN CORGI BOOKS

Novels

☐	552 07981 2	THE GAMES	*Hugh Atkinson*	7/6
☐	552 07763 1	ANOTHER COUNTRY	*James Baldwin*	5/–
☐	552 07982 0	SEVENTH AVENUE	*Norman Bogner*	7/6
☐	552 07885 9	CONFESSIONS OF A SPENT YOUTH	*Vance Bourjaily*	7/6
☐	552 07938 3	THE NAKED LUNCH	*William Burroughs*	7/6
☐	552 08042 X	LORD DISMISS US	*Michael Campbell*	7/6
☐	552 07317 6	THE CHINESE ROOM	*Vivian Connell*	5/–
☐	552 07777 1	THE WAR BABIES	*Gwen Davis*	5/–
☐	552 01278 5	THE GINGER MAN	*J. P. Donleavy*	5/–
☐	552 07488 8	BOYS AND GIRLS TOGETHER	*William Goldman*	7/6
☐	552 07968 5	THE WELL OF LONELINESS	*Radclyffe Hall*	7/6
☐	552 01500 8	CATCH–22	*Joseph Heller*	5/–
☐	552 07904 9	THE CONSULTANT	*Alec Hilton*	5/–
☐	552 08054 3	PINKTOES	*Chester Himes*	5/–
☐	552 07193 5	MOTHERS AND DAUGHTERS	*Evan Hunter*	7/6
☐	552 08043 8	TO SEE A FINE LADY	*Norah Lofts*	5/–
☐	552 07779 8	THE DEER PARK	*Norman Mailer*	5/–
☐	552 08002 0	MY SISTER, MY BRIDE	*Edwina Mark*	5/–
☐	552 08015 2	FLESH AND BLOOD	*Nan Maynard*	4/–
☐	552 07594 9	HAWAII (colour illustrations)	*James A. Michener*	10/6
☐	552 07500 0	THE SOURCE	*James A. Michener*	12/6
☐	552 01066 9	LOLITA	*Vladimir Nabokov*	5/–
☐	552 07766 6	APPOINTMENT IN SAMARRA	*John O'Hara*	5/–
☐	552 07954 5	RUN FOR THE TREES	*James Rand*	7/6
☐	552 01162 2	A STONE FOR DANNY FISHER	*Harold Robbins*	5/–
☐	552 07655 4	THE HONEY BADGER	*Robert Ruark*	7/6
☐	552 08022 5	THE DEVIL'S SUMMER	*Edmund Schiddel*	7/6
☐	552 07807 7	VALLEY OF THE DOLLS	*Jacqueline Susann*	7/6
☐	552 07883 2	THE CARETAKERS	*Dariel Telfer*	5/–
☐	552 07921 9	THE BASTARD Vol. I	*Brigitte von Tessin*	5/–
☐	552 07922 7	THE BASTARD Vol. II	*Brigitte von Tessin*	7/6
☐	552 07937 5	THE DETECTIVE	*Roderick Thorp*	7/6
☐	552 07352 0	EXODUS	*Leon Uris*	7/6
☐	552 08041 1	THE NIGHT IS A TIME FOR LISTENING	*Elliot West*	5/–
☐	552 07116 1	FOREVER AMBER Vol. I	*Kathleen Winsor*	5/–
☐	552 07117 X	FOREVER AMBER Vol. II	*Kathleen Winsor*	5/–
☐	552 07998 7	THE TROJANS	*Wirt Williams*	7/6
☐	552 07790 9	THE BEFORE MIDNIGHT SCHOLAR	*Li Yu*	7/6

War

☐	552 07936 7	THE DEVIL'S BRIGADE	*George Walton and Robert Adleman*	5/–
☐	552 08031 4	THE LONG GREEN TUNNEL	*Hew Crawford*	3/6
☐	552 08003 9	ESCAPE FROM GERMANY	*Aidan Crawley*	5/–
☐	552 08045 4	NOTHING IMPORTANT EVER DIES	*Romain Gary*	3/6
☐	552 07871 9	COMRADES OF WAR	*Sven Hassel*	5/–
☐	552 07959 6	THREE CAME HOME	*Agnes Keith*	5/–
☐	552 07986 3	HIROSHIMA REEF	*Eric Lambert*	5/–
☐	552 07726 7	THE DIRTY DOZEN	*E. M. Nathanson*	7/6
☐	552 07910 3	THE GERMAN ARMY AND THE NAZI PARTY (illustrated)	*Robert J. O'Neill*	7/6
☐	552 07476 4	THE SCOURGE OF THE SWASTIKA (illustrated)	*Lord Russell of Liverpool*	5/–
☐	552 07997 9	THE UNFEELING SKY	*Peter Saxon*	3/6

Romance

☐	552 07947 2	STORM CASTLE	*Jan Andersen*	3/6
☐	552 08036 5	THE NEW SISTER THEATRE	*Lucilla Andrews*	3/6
☐	552 08050 0	THE DOCTORS OF DOWNLANDS	*Sheila Brandon*	3/6
☐	552 08008 X	THE NIGHT IS KIND	*Bess Norton*	3/6
☐	552 08051 9	JUNGLE NURSE	*Irene Roberts*	3/6

Science Fiction

☐ 552 08037 3	NEW WRITINGS IN S.F.13	*John Carnell*	3/6
☐ 552 07860 3	THE MENACE FROM EARTH	*Robert Heinlein*	3/6
☐ 552 07994 4	THE OTHER FOOT	*Damon Knight*	3/6
☐ 552 07682 1	THE SHAPE OF THINGS TO COME	*H. G. Wells*	7/6
☐ 552 08052 7	DEADLY LITTER	*James White*	3/6

General

☐ 552 07704 6	THE VIRILITY DIET	*Dr. George Belham*	5/–
☐ 552 07566 3	SEXUAL LIFE IN ENGLAND	*Dr. Ivan Bloch*	9/6
☐ 552 08009 8	THE PLEASURES OF LOVE	*Barbara Bross*	7/6
☐ 552 07593 0	UNMARRIED LOVE	*Dr. Eustace Chesser*	5/–
☐ 552 07949 9	GROW UP—AND LIVE	*Dr. Eustace Chesser*	3/6
☐ 552 07951 0	YOU MUST HAVE LOVE	*Dr. Eustace Chesser*	3/6
☐ 552 07996 0	THE ISLAND RACE (fully illustrated in colour)	*Winston S. Churchill*	30/–
☐ 552 07924 3	BARBARELLA (illustrated)	*Jean Claude Forest*	12/6
☐ 552 07804 2	THE BIRTH CONTROLLERS	*Peter Fryer*	7/6
☐ 552 07400 4	MY LIFE AND LOVES	*Frank Harris*	12/6
☐ 552 07745 3	COWBOY KATE (illustrated)	*Sam Haskins*	21/–
☐ 552 01541 5	MAN AND SEX	*Kaufman and Borgeson*	5/–
☐ 552 07916 2	SEXUAL RESPONSE IN WOMEN	*Drs. E. and P. Kronhausen*	9/6
☐ 552 07820 4	THE CATHOLIC MARRIAGE	*William A. Lynch*	5/–
☐ 552 07965 0	SOHO NIGHT AND DAY (illustrated)	*Frank Norman and Jeffrey Bernard*	7/6
☐ 552 07145 5	THE THIRD EYE	*Lobsang Rampa*	5/–
☐ 552 08038 1	EROS DENIED (illustrated)	*Wayland Young*	7/6
☐ 552 07918 9	BRUCE TEGNER'S COMPLETE BOOK OF KARATE (illustrated)		6/–

Westerns

☐ 552 08049 7	SINGING GUNS	*Max Brand*	3/6
☐ 552 08006 3	TIMBAL GULCH TRAIL	*Max Brand*	3/6
☐ 552 07976 6	SUDDEN AT BAY	*Frederick H. Christian*	3/6
☐ 552 08021 7	THE FASTEST GUN IN TEXAS, No. 30	*J. T. Edson*	3/6
☐ 552 08019 5	THE LAW OF THE GUN, No. 28	*J. T. Edson*	3/6
☐ 552 08048 9	THE PROFESSIONAL KILLERS	*J. T. Edson*	3/6
☐ 552 08034 9	THE LAST WARPATH	*Will Henry*	5/–
☐ 552 08035 7	BRIONNE	*Louis L'Amour*	3/6
☐ 552 07902 2	SHALAKO	*Louis L'Amour*	3/6
☐ 552 08007 1	CHANCY	*Louis L'Amour*	3/6

Crime

☐ 552 07872 7	THE KREMLIN LETTER	*Noel Behn*	5/–
☐ 552 07974 X	PHOTO FINISH	*Jean Bruce*	3/6
☐ 552 07855 7	STRIP TEASE	*Jean Bruce*	3/6
☐ 552 08032 2	DOOMSDAY ENGLAND	*Michael Cooney*	5/–
☐ 552 08063 2	THE DARK CIRCLE	*John Creasey*	3/6
☐ 552 08005 5	DOUBLE FOR DEATH	*John Creasey*	3/6
☐ 552 07912 X	WIDOWS WEAR WEEDS	*A. A. Fair (Erle Stanley Gardner)*	3/6
☐ 552 07716 X	AMBER NINE	*John Gardner*	3/6
☐ 552 08004 7	MADRIGAL	*John Gardner*	5/–
☐ 552 07905 7	HIDEAWAY	*John Gardner*	3/6
☐ 552 08033 0	MR. SCIPIO	*Tudor Gates*	3/6
☐ 552 07988 X	UNDERCOVER CAT PROWLS AGAIN	*The Gordons*	3/6
☐ 552 07677 5	DIE RICH, DIE HAPPY	*James Munro*	3/6
☐ 552 07973 1	THE BODY LOVERS	*Mickey Spillane*	4/–
☐ 552 07831 X	THE BY-PASS CONTROL	*Mickey Spillane*	3/6

All these books are available at your bookshop or newsagent: or can be ordered direct from the publisher. Just tick the titles you want and fill in the form below.

CORGI BOOKS, Cash Sales Department, J. Barnicoat (Falmouth) Ltd., P.O. Box 11, Falmouth, Cornwall.

Please send cheque or postal order. No currency, and allow 6d. per book to cover the cost of postage and packing in U.K., 9d. per copy overseas.

NAME ______________________________

ADDRESS ______________________________

(DEC. 68)______________________________